MOUNTAIN MEMORIES II

Book II

by
J. Dennis Deitz

With a Foreword by
David A. Bice

Illustrated by
Steve Harrison

Third Printing
Mountain Memories
216 Sutherland Drive,
South Charleston, WV 25303
© 1983 J. Dennis Deitz
Printed in The United States of America
Library of Congress Number 83-080178
ISBN 0-934750-18-1

Dedicated to

Madeline Deitz

**Front Cover Illustration
of the Deitz Farm
in 1983**

Table of Contents

FOREWARD

There are many people who say time after time, "I should write a book about that." Most never do. MOUNTAIN MEMORIES II is the result, though, of a man who did write his book. Dennis Deitz has not pretended to be a great writer, only a recollecter of times past. He has observed the first rule of good writing, that is to write from the author's viewpoint and write only that which he knows about. Second, he has written for his audience and not down to it. Mr. Deitz has recounted the stories of his youth and working years just as if he were talking face to face with the reader.

The stories contained in this book serve two purposes. First, they preserve the past for a rapidly changing society. Second, they lead the reader into recollections. Each reader will begin to remember stories which have lain dormant in the shadows of his or her mind. Perhaps, the awakened memories will cause the reader to record these thoughts for the rest of us. Nothing would make Mr. Deitz happier than for this book to "set fire" to another unknown author, who will help lead us down the path of our past.

DAVID A. BICE

INTRODUCTION

In writing this book I am mostly describing the deceased members of my family as I knew them and from a personal viewpoint, not from the viewpoint of any of my living brothers and sisters. I am not writing about some of my brothers and sisters as they are private people and do not choose to be pictured individually, so I respect their wishes, but I wish to say all of them are fine people, and we have a very close family group. All of my nieces and nephews are also close to all of us.

I will briefly describe the family genealogy as we descend from the very earliest settlers in almost every family line in what is now the state of West Virginia. I show this background because of my family research. My family doesn't fit the description of the earlier settlers written about by some authors who apparently spent some time in the Appalachian Mountains and became "experts" in analyzing the inhabitants. These writers would have you believe every early settler came from the same place overseas as the other settlers, and their descendants ended up in a shack today, living on welfare. This just isn't so. Most of the descendants of the early settlers I have researched have done well and are still hard working, honest people. This includes hundreds of cousins and allied cousins. I have not found any who collected unemployment benefits as most of these people either found another job locally or migrated to where they could find employment. Some created jobs for themselves.

West Virginia does have a large share of people on welfare and/or food stamps. Almost all of them descend from people who came to this country later to work in the coal mines or the timber industry. They surrendered when work got slack.

Descendants of the first settlers I know still seem to have kept their old sense of independence from their forebears and refused to be beholden to anyone or the government.

Part of their refusal to accept something for nothing was from their basic sense of honesty, and part was from a sense of independence. They just totally refused to take anything they hadn't earned or did not want anything they hadn't earned. The only exception to this was during illness. If a neighbor was sick, everyone in the community (in the old days) helped to plant his crops, cultivate them, and then harvest them. In turn, an ill person accepted this help as a way of life. People traded labor with each other as needed. Their independence came from their pioneer background. They had migrated into the wilderness, even back to the days of the Indians, cleared ground, planted crops, raised flax, and kept sheep. The pioneer wives spun this wool and flax into cloth and then sewed and knitted the cloth into clothes. Shoes were made from leather they had tanned from skins of animals they had killed. They killed wild game, which was abundant, for food and clothes, and they raised and bred their own farm animals. They bartered or traded for any extra things they needed, using their farm products or furs as the medium of exchange.

Land was obtained in about as many ways as there weré people. One of my earliest ancestors in West Virginia was William McClung, who came to western Greenbrier County about 1760 and made a "tomahawk" claim of 100,000 acres, or almost the entire Meadow River basin. Apparently, most of this claim stood up against other claims. He gave his descendants thousands of acres as they married and started families. His daughter-in-law, Mary Alderson McClung, (my great, great grandmother) rode horseback alone to Richmond to obtain a claim of several thousand acres in what is now the Mt. Lookout community. She gave deeds to her nieces and nephews and later to her children and grandchildren for four hundred acres each. This was how this community was first settled, and this was why my great grandfather, John Deitz, came to settle there. He was the son-in-law of Mary Alderson McClung and came there in the early 1830's.

Many early settlers bought land in Nicholas County for a few dollars per acre, but some early settlers picked out a likely site for a home with a spring nearby, built a cabin, cleared land for farming, and did not know at the time who the owner was. It might be several years before the owner came and claimed the land. The settler usually bought the land if a price could be agreed upon. If not, the settler might move his family farther west to other unoccupied land and build another cabin and clear more land.

A lot of this land, maybe thousands of acres, was bought by land investors sight unseen. When the original settler obtained title to a lot of acreage, he would give his children enough land for farms. The families were so large that after one or two generations there would not be enough land for the descendants, so they either had to buy land or migrate further west. In my work in genealogy, I have corresponded with many distant cousins and have accumulated the stories of many relatives who migrated further west where land grants would still be obtained. Several of these relatives have kept the family histories. One of these was my father's grandmother's family named Corron. Almost all of her brothers and sisters migrated to Niles, Michigan, but one brother, Robert Corron, then migrated to near Elgin, Illinois, in 1834. As he traveled west, he saw a large brick house on a hilltop in West Virginia, and he remarked that if he prospered in the new land he would build a house just like that one. In 1850 he started the new home, making bricks from his new land. His grandson, also Robert Corron, still lives in this home. I have pictures of this beautiful house.

His sister, Rachel, also moved to Illinois with her husband, Jacob Amick. This country in Illinois still had Indians living there. One time the Indians came into her cabin and took her bread from the open fireplace where it was cooking. Rachel's and Jacob's son, Myron, was a famous Civil War scout.

There are other interesting stories told about and by the descendants of the people who migrated west.

I asked my nephew, Larry Deitz, to write about his grandmother from the standpoint of one of the grandchildren who had been with her as a child, more than my children. Larry did a wonderful job, and I appreciate his writing this accolade to his grandmother.

Writing a book makes an author dependent on other people. Contrary to popular belief one does not sit down to a typewriter and instantly produce the great American novel. Other people aid in many ways. Kathleen Browning has aided me at every turn and comma. She was invaluable in editing this work and even typed the final manuscript. When there was a word which needed to be changed or a thought clarified, Kathleen was always there with her assistance. Ruth Edwards and Annette Barnette also helped with proofreading.

PREFACE

The stories on the following pages are written with loving care about tender memories of family, friends, neighbors, and a section of Appalachia where the people were descendants of settlers who came into the wilderness immediately after the Revolutionary War. These people were brave, industrious and hardy, and they had a spirit of adventure and independence which characterized the pioneers in America.

One pioneer lived in a cave until a cabin was built, and one ancestor rode horseback to Richmond from what is now Greenbrier County to get a land grant of thousands of acres, which she divided among family members.

Conditions which would be considered intolerable handicaps today were accepted stoically, while the people strove to make a better life for themselves in the wild uncultivated and uninhabitated region. It is true there was abundant land, the soil was good for farming, and the forests of virgin timber seemed endless, but the land had to be cleared of this timber before farming could begin, so the trees were cut by axes and burned so as to have farming land. The roots of the trees were a nuisance too, so a root-cutter plow was developed. The infinite ingenuity of these people to develop tools to meet their needs is legendary.

The freedom from too many legal restraints in the old countries was valued, but these people also valued law and order. There was not much delinquency among them.

The churches were few and far between, but the religious feelings were combined with social needs to make the church a binding force in their quality of life.

Subscription schools were established if a teacher could be found, and the boys were sent, for the education of girls was spinning, weaving, candle making and the other multitude of household chores required to keep a large family clothed, fed and from freezing in the severe winters.

The medical needs were met largely through herbs and general knowledge as to how to meet sickness. Babies were born at home, and bones were set there too. These people, our ancestors, were firecely independent and proud of being able to meet their own needs, but they freely gave and received help in times of adversity.

KATHLEEN BROWNING

BOYHOOD MEMORIES

STEVE HARRISON

BOYHOOD MOUNTAIN MEMORIES

Our farm of something over 100 acres, most of it cleared flat land with good soil, lay on Hickory Flats Ridge in Greenbrier and Nicholas Counties. At one end of the flat land was a knob field, which could also be farmed. From the knob field, which had an elevation of three thousand feet above sea level, a person could see as far as the eye could carry except along the Hickory Flats Ridge. There was a beautiful view in any season of the year. If there was any wind blowing, we had wind, for there was nothing to slow the prevailing winds this side of the Rocky Mountains.

I remember the sleet which sometimes hit. It would cover every branch of the bare trees. From the top of our hill, as far as you could see, it looked like a forest of crystal trees. If the sun came out and reflected on them, it would look like a cut glass, crystal world as far as you could see.

Sometimes, through the years, I have seen people proudly show off beautiful glassware and think, "I have stood on top of a West Virginia mountain and have seen the whole world, as far as I could see, look like that."

Sometimes there would be a constant roar of breaking limbs from the weight of the ice as it melted.

The house where I grew up stood about 500 feet below the knob field on a natural bench, a perfect setting for a house, and it was about 100 yards from the country road. The house built by my Grandfather Isaac Nutter had burned, and a new ten room house was built the year I was born and is still standing. Most of the joists and framing were built of chestnut lumber, and there was oak flooring.

Great, great Grandfather David Nutter had come to Laurel Creek in Nicholas County from Monroe County in 1814, so the Nutter family had been in Nicholas County for 99 years before I was born.

The post office and telephone central were in our house, so we were in contact with many people on the phone and had lots of company because of people coming to get their mail.

As we sat around the roaring fire, I remember the winds

sometimes making a loud whistling sound around the eaves of the house. It gave me a safe, comfortable feeling to be in our warm living room, but this warmth did not extend beyond the living room and kitchen too much on winter days. The feather ticks, which were mattress sized and shaped sacks made of a blue and white striped material and filled with feathers, were warm, but only after you were in them long enough to get them warm. The feathers fluffed up around our bodies to meet the quilts and formed an insulation. We only used the feather ticks in the winter as they were too hot in the summer.

When I was five or six years old, three or four of the younger children would sleep in one bed in the winter like spoons, facing the same direction. When we wanted to turn over, someone would say "spoon," and everyone would turn the other way.

Life around our fireplace was really interesting as our farm was where everyone stopped for the night when traveling through the country. If we saw a man ride his horse up to the barn, take off the saddle and feed the horse, then we knew we were going to have a guest for the night. There would be county officials, cattle and sheep buyers, tax collectors, and circuit riders visiting and staying with us. Sometimes owners of huge acreage of timber and coal lands from New York or Boston stopped at our house, but most of these men stayed with Grandfather Nutter, as he was a surveyor for them.

Great discussions took place. Some of these people might not have had too much formal education, but they were self-educated. They were all readers of newspapers and magazines, and they analyzed what they read.

Most of the time, as I grew up, we received a daily paper through the mail, and magazines too. It was difficult to bring up anything which my parents hadn't read about. Many of our visitors were at the lower end of the education and knowledge scale, but Dad was the most democratic person in the world, and he treated the most ignorant bum exactly like he treated the most prominent person--with the same hospitality. Some of these people were real characters, and their speech and ideas might be like no one else in the world. I had a buddy who could imitate any of them exactly in speech and manner.

Almost no one in my family and none of the neighbors

believed in ghost stories or omens, but some of these visitors did, and some of their ghost stories could make my hair stand on end, making my trip upstairs to bed a scary experience, even if I didn't believe the stories. Most of these men believed every word of every story they told, and they were convincing.

Dennis Deitz at age five, 1918

Walking along those country roads at night through the woods, with bright moonlight shining through the trees, it was easy to see why they thought they had seen ghosts. The moonlight would shine through openings between the branches of the trees on to old stumps, rocks and tree trunks, and a shape might be seen which could resemble anything from a headless woman to a bear. When a person got to it, with many a reluctant step, it might prove to be something very ordinary. However, there was a wildcat, which had a den in a rock cliff across from our farm house, and many a time during my return home at night, the wildcat would let out one blood curdling scream after another. I always found it impossible to walk slowly, no matter how hard I tried, for at times like this, my mind had trouble convincing my feet they weren't scared.

During the winter my Father always kept a roaring fire of wood or coal. Our chores ended early because of the early darkness, and we would eat a big warm supper and sit around the fire. When the neighbors came for their mail we talked, and we loved this and other company too. We would look down the road to see if anyone was walking up the road carrying a lantern, because if we saw the light we would know we were to have a visitor or someone coming to get the mail. Then we might have someone to play checkers with. If no one came, Dad and I might play checkers. School mates often stayed all night with us, and my sisters would boil chestnuts or make candy or popcorn. We might play hide and seek or blind man's bluff.

I especially remember the long cold journey from the bedroom in the morning to the fireplace to dress. The boys' bedroom was the far upstairs bedroom, and in the winter the room was probably about as cold as the outside. I would be sleeping in my underclothes, and when I was called, I would lie in the warm bed for a few minutes, planning the dash from the bed to the fireplace--where to grab my clothes and shoes, how to make the trip through the upper hallway, down the stairs, through the lower hallway, and to the fireplace to dress. I would try to save a few inches of distance on each corner. The jump from the bed to the floor was like jumping into a cold icy pool.

On arriving at the fireplace I must have looked like a spinning top, trying to get every side warm at once. After I had warmed up and dressed, my Father might come in and make one of his winter time remarks, like "How would you like to be standing on that windy knob with nothing on but a wet sheet around you?" If you dwelled on that question, it would almost set your teeth to chattering

4

again. Or he might say, "It's so cold out there that when I threw a pan of boiling water out, it froze so fast into ice that the ice was still hot."

We had running water in the house on the farm as early as 1925. The water was piped from a spring on the hill through glavanized pipe for about 500 feet. We also had a hot water tank in the kitchen, but there was not a bathroom in the house. The water for the hot water tank was heated through the kitchen stove in a special liner which was placed in the firebox in the cook stove, and water from the hot water tank was piped into the special liner, back to the tank, and then to the kitchen sink. Thus, there was hot water when a fire was built in the cook stove.

On one of our many cold winter nights, the pipes which led to this liner froze. When my Father built a fire in the stove and came back to add fuel to the fire, the steam had built up in this liner, and, not being able to escape through the frozen pipes, built up pressure and blew out the whole end of the cook stove. My Father was standing next to it and was blown across the room, but he was not hurt too much. This was the only heater of this type I ever saw. I think we had a very cold breakfast that morning.

One neighbor living about two miles across the hills claimed to have heard the explosion, even though it didn't awaken the sleeping children.

Although life was rugged and hard, it was also fun and interesting. It was almost fun on the run. We had to create fun while we were working hard in the evenings and Sunday. There was no organized fun outside of school or church. You did what you could between chores, such as running a trap line, hunting squirrels or rabbits after the farm work was done. When one of my school mates came home with me to stay all night, he would help with my chores, and this might leave extra time for hunting or trapping, or, if it was in the fall, we would gather all types of nuts, such as chestnuts, hickory nuts, and both black and white walnuts. The white walnuts, as we called them, were actually butternuts.

The chores on the farm were mostly divided by need. The eight of us who grew to adulthood covered a span of twenty years in our age differences. When I was nine to fifteen years old, I was the only working age boy at home. Most of my work was outside work, such as helping to feed the farm animals, checking on the animals in the fields, chopping wood and carrying in the wood and coal.

Farm life required every member of the family to work early and late if everyone was to eat, stay warm and survive.

My favorite job on the farm was looking after the sheep. It was my job on the way to and from school to go to a large flat field on top of the hill and check on about forty to fifty sheep and account for all of them. I recognized all of them and gave them names of people I knew, imagining some facial similarity.

I checked on the sheep every morning and afternoon where they fed on racks filled with straw and hay, and I counted them to see that they were still safe from dogs or hadn't been smothered where they fed on the bottoms of haystacks. Sometimes they might eat to the stack pole, which allowed the rest of the hay to slide down the pole and smother them. Usually we kept this type of haystack away from the sheep.

My sisters did the milking and also helped in the kitchen and with the other housework. They also helped when the potatoes were dug and gathered and in the garden in the summer. All of us picked berries in season, along with the cherries and apples. These things had to be done in a hurry when they were ripe or when the ground was dry.

We usually had a live-in hired man or girl during the fall and spring season when there was so much work to be done, and my Father was teaching and only had Saturdays off.

Mom and Dad were the parents of nine children. All survived except for Pearl, next to me, who died with spinal meningitis when she was five years old. Four boys and four girls grew to adulthood. In order of age, we were Granville, Faye, Lawrence, Irene, Helen, Dennis, Pearl, Murrel and Harold.

I think winter was my favorite time of the year. The view from the top mountain field was sometimes stark and harsh as the trees were naked and maybe dreary, but there were days when they appeared magnificent. Sometimes the winds would be fierce in this field, with the wind and snow blowing all the way from the Rocky Mountains, as there was no higher elevation between the Rockies and this Greenbrier County mountain country.

Many times the snow would be blowing completely sideways in great gusts. I was a skinny little boy, but I could easily imagine that I was fighting the battle of man against the elements.

I was a voracious reader, especially of the old mountain men of the west. From this mountain field I could look in one direction and see nothing but wild, spectacular mountains without a sign of habitation. It was easy to imagine being Kit Carson or Jim Bridger in the Rockies, looking and seeing where no white man had ever been before. If I could see a little smoke, that would, of course, be Indian camp fires. I would sometimes step out of the broken paths to see what it was like and would trip, landing on my back and bottom and slide until something stopped me. This caused me to have many bumps, bruises and skinned up parts.

Sometimes deep snow would fall, followed by a warm day, and the top of the snow would melt. Then another cold night might follow, making the top an icy crust. When the sun would shine, this could leave the whole country under the shining sun just sparkling icy snow, glistening as far as you could see.

Some of these cold winter days the snow would be blowing sideways, driven by almost constant wind. I would be dressed to keep warm, and I loved a day like that. Maybe I was just different, or maybe it was the man against nature atmosphere, or maybe I was just looking forward to our always maintained big fire in the grate and a warm supper to go with it.

My Father's favorite season was fall, but spring was Mom's favorite time of the year. She loved to see the earth come to life again. Spring in the mountains was different from spring in the valleys. The redbud, service and dogwood bloomed before the leaves appeared on the trees. These, along with ground flowers, showed up so much more than when the young green leaves came out at the same time and covered them.

By spring our green canned food supplies were low, and I began to really hunger for fresh green vegetables — it seemed forever before they arrived. By April we could find wild morel mushrooms, and we would have green winter onions and wild creasy greens. The green beans were what I was really starved for, but I had to wait till summer for

7

them.

In the early spring we started preparing the fields for planting of most crops by plowing. The level fields were turned with a turning plow going around the outside and working toward the center, turning the sod to the bottom, with the deep soil ending up on top. The hillside fields were turned with a hillside plow, starting at the bottom of the field and working to the top. The hillside plow had a mold board which could be reversed, that is, in going in one direction the soil would turn down hill. At end of the field the mold board would reverse, and going the opposite way the soil would still turn down hill.

Next, a harrow[1] would be used to break up the soil into finer, more granular beds for seed. The harrows were home made of about six inch by six inch wooden pieces about eight feet long, shaped like the letter A. Square iron spikes about one inch by one inch and twelve inches long would be placed through the wooden pieces about every eight or ten inches. This was done by boring under size holes and then using heated iron spikes to partially drive the spikes through the holes, causing the holes to be square to fit the square teeth for the harrow. An iron hook or ring was attached to the apex of the A. Here the double tree could be attached so the horses could be hooked up to pull the harrow. Sometimes an extra cross piece was added. You then either rode on the harrow or walked beside it and drove the team over the plowed area again and again. Sometimes the field might then be dragged with a home made drag. The drag would be made by using two pieces of timber exactly like two sled runners. Boards would be nailed to the bottom of the runners, starting with the back end, with each board lapping on the next one, making it run a littler better.

The soil was now ready for the cereal crops.

If you were planting a garden, potato or corn furrows would have to be made and seed dropped and covered with a hoe. The furrows were made by a single shovel plow pulled by a horse. The shovel plow might also be made with an upright piece of wood about 5"x5"x3' long with a metal plow bolted to the bottom curved point, which

[1]Sometimes called a peg-toothed harrow.

8

would be 8" high and 6" wide. A piece of wood, the beam, similar to the upright piece, was attached parallel to the ground, to the upright piece. At the front end of this was a clevice or open ring, to hook the single tree for the horse to pull. Of course, handles were attached to the upright piece in order to guide the plow.

It was usually my job to ride the horse to pull the plow and keep the rows straight.

After the potatoes and corn came up, we used a cultivator to keep the weeds out, cultivating one row at a time. The cultivators were usually bought and had about ten small plow points attached.

In order to plant potatoes, rows were laid off. We cut seed potatoes by cutting a potato in four or five pieces, leaving at least two eyes in each piece. Two or three pieces were dropped to a hill, about two or three feet apart, and covered with two or three inches of dirt. These formed what we called potato hills. The potatoes were hoed until they bloomed and the tops died. After several weeks the potatoes were dug by going through with the shovel plow several times. The potatoes were picked up by hand. To store them for the winter, we dug a hole on a slope several feet across, placed a lot of straw in the bottom, filled it with potatoes, covering them with several more inches of straw. That was then covered with several inches of dirt and boards or roofing to make the rains run off. A ditch was dug around this mound to carry off the water and keep it out.

Corn was planted in hills. If we planted on level ground, furrows were laid off both ways, with the rows about three feet apart and three or four kernels of corn per hill. We could run the cultivator both ways, cutting down the hoeing. The seed was covered about two inches deep. After the corn came up, it was thinned. Then the corn had to be hoed. Sometimes Dad, a brother and a hired man would be with me, but sometimes I would have the whole field to myself. This was the worst!

When the corn was about waist high, it was laid aside, meaning that it no longer had to be worked.

Corn field beans might be planted along with the corn, the corn stalks serving as supports for the beans. Pumpkins might be planted among the corn stalks. When the corn ripened, it was cut. This was done by tying stalks

9

from four hills being bent toward the center and tied together. All of the near corn would be cut with a short handled corn cutter by hand and stood upright in these supports, and a string was tied around the shock of corn. After it dried for a few weeks, it would be hauled to a central spot and shucked there.

A shucking peg was made by whittling a piece of hickory wood into the size and shape of a forefinger, maybe a little sharper on the front end, a leather strap would be cut, with two holes, one in each end. The holes fitted into the grooves snugly, forming a loop in the leather to fit over the middle finger. This was to keep from losing the shucking peg while opening and closing the hand.

The sharp end of the peg was used to grab into the open end of the corn shuck and peel it away in two quick motions. Bushels of corn might be shucked or peeled in one day. The corn would be stored in the corn cribs with side slats having openings between them to allow air to circulate. The corn fodder would be stored in the barn and fed to the farm animals during the winter. Corn had to be shelled for the chickens every day, and some of the ears had small briery, rough ends on the outside. Was it ever hard on the inside bottoms of your thumbs! The corn shellers which came later were a great invention.

There was a tradition concerning corn–it you found a red ear you could kiss a pretty girl of your choice. What a horrible idea at ten, and what a wonderful idea at twenty!

Corn, wheat and buckwheat usually were planted in the prepared fields by a horse drawn drill, allowing the seed to be planted two or three inches deep, along with the fertilizer. These crops could be left until they ripened before cutting. Our land was too rough and small to be cut by reapers, so they were cradled by hand. A cradle looked like a scythe except that there were four fingers attached so that they were parallel to the scythe cutting blade, being about three feet wide. The cradler would take a full length arm swing, in such a way as to leave the grain cradled in the cradle. The cradler continued the motion toward ground behind him and lay the grain on the ground. Behind him he would leave a row of cut grain in a continuous row, almost perfectly even, with the grain heads in the same direction.

The rakes we used to rake the grain into sheaves were

home made, and the handles were six or seven feet long. A hole was drilled into a cross piece of wood to fit the handle. Pieces of flexible hickory were fitted into holes in the top of the cross piece through a hole in the handle and back in the other end of the cross piece. Three or four of these would be used to support the handle to the cross piece. Then holes would be drilled into the bottom of the cross piece, and six inch wooden teeth placed in them. I was the right age to be the raker. I would reach the rake out full length and pull the grain into sheaves. If the remaining stubble was extra dry or strong, it would really be hard on bare feet.

Next came the tying of the sheaves. You would walk, grab a sheaf, take a couple of dozen straws and tie the sheaf in the middle, throw it to a center spot for a dozen sheaves and never stop walking. A dozen sheaves would be stood on the butt ends, with two used for caps, broken and spread in the middle, to act as a roof for the shocks.

These sheaves dried for a while. When it came time to thresh the grain, the sheaves would be upset, with butt ends toward the sun to dry a day or two before storing. They might be stored in the barn or be made into stacks.

If the threshing machine was coming at the time the shocks were still dry in the field, they could be hauled directly to the thresher from the field. The threshing machine owner would thresh the grain for a toll or percentage of the crop. All of the farmers would trade labor, or the son's labor, and go from farm to farm.

My first job was to hold sacks for the worker, catching the grain and pouring it into the sacks. I was lining the sheaves up along a table for the worker who fed the thresher, grain end first, after cutting the tie bands with a knife. One time I was lining the sheaves, pushing them toward the cutter, when he was grabbing and cutting, and he cut my knuckles instead. I still have the scar.

The grain would be stored in bins in the barn. Most of it we used for animal feed as we usually bought flour and meal by the barrel, although I have taken some to the mill to be ground.

Our hay seed was usually planted along with the wheat and oats, but it would not really get started until the second year, when we would get a crop of hay. We then used a horse drawn mowing machine, although small rough fields might be cut with a scythe. I remember Dad using a scythe and have to stop often to whet the scythe with a whet rock. He could almost play a tune with the whet rock on the blade as he sharpened it.

After the hay was cut, it had to stay on the ground a day or so to cure and dry before it could be put into shocks. If the rains fell at this point for an extended period, the hay would mold and spoil. Yet, it had to be cut when it ripened. After it had dried for a day or two, a horse drawn hay rake was used to rake it into windrows, parallel to each other. Then pitchforks were used to make the windrows into shocks of about five feet high and five feet across. Here the hay stayed for further curing before either being hauled to the haymows or made into haystacks.

We might haul it to the barn mows (lofts) in a wagon with a special rack placed on the wagon to hold a large quantity. There it would be thrown into the mows with a pitchfork. A worker in the hay mow would then throw it further back, and I was the one to tramp it down to make more room. This was one hot, dusty job, but one I was well qualified to do as it required more feet than head.

In making a haystack, a pole about twenty feet long was put into the ground and small wooden supports were driven into the ground at angles and nailed to the upright pole, and the haystack was started. If the stack was near the shocks, I usually hauled the shocks to the stack. I would use a horse and a long log chain, hooking one end to the single tree behind the horse, placing the chain around the shock and along the side, putting the chain underneath the shock. Then I would hook the other end of the chain to the single tree and pull the shock to the stack. The stack might be twelve feet across and fifteen to twenty feet high, looking like the top half of a football cut in half.

I don't really remember the first chores that were required of me as there were so many, enough for everyone and then a lot left over. I suppose my first jobs were to bring small items and tools. A little later it would be carrying water and coal, then carrying water to the workers in the fields. Always things had to be taken to my Nutter grandparents' place, or I would have to go there after something.

All of this was hard on bare feet. I would stump my toes on rocks and often lose toenails. In the fall I stepped on chestnut burrs. Sometimes it seemed a hundred stickers would be left in my instep. I just never developed tough skin on the soles of my feet as did a lot of my buddies. I have seen them with skin so thick on the bottoms of their feet they could stomp chestnuts out of the burrs. Not me. My high instep would always stay tender.

Later I split wood and carried it into the house. Did we ever use wood! Although we also used coal, the way my Dad liked a hot fire, we used wood by the cord very quickly.

We had a great wood supply. On the opposite side of the hill, the land had been timbered, leaving trees six to twelve inches across. Then a fire had burned through, killing the trees, but leaving them standing where they dried out. Then a few top limbs could be cut out with an axe, and the tree could be snaked (dragged) out to a flat field. The tree trunk could then be cut into the right lengths and stored in our thirty by thirty foot wood shed. We could split them into kindling as they were needed.

Most of our fences were made by splitting chestnut timber. There was a lot of long, straight chestnut timber in our Hickory Flats country. Even after the blight killed the chestnut trees, the standing dead trees dried out and still

Watson and Betty Deitz, their daughters and Dennis, 1923

13

made good rails for a number of years.

The trees were cut by chopping a notch on the side or direction you wanted the trees to fall. Then a crosscut saw was used by two men on the opposite side, sawing toward the notch. If it would bind, a wedge was driven into the saw cut and hit with a sledge hammer, letting the saw run free, and the sawing continued. When the tree fell, the side limbs would be cut by an axe, and the logs were cut into proper lengths and snaked or pulled to a good working spot by a team of horses. There they would be split into rails. This was done by driving a couple of wedges into one end. As the log started to split, another iron wedge would be driven into the side split. Then locust gluts (wooden wedges) would be driven into the split until the log split into two halves. Then one half would be split the same way in two quarters. That would be split until it was the right size for rails. The rails would be hauled by wagon to the field to be fenced. Usually we built snake fences, that is, one rail was laid down, the next rail laid crosswise at the end of the first; the next rail laid the opposite direction at the end of the second. Overall, it made a straight line until a corner was desired. We usually laid the rails seven rails high.

A five acre field could be fenced in two or three days. Many people could split three to four hundred rails per day. I was not old enough to be a rail splitter before the chestnut timber was gone. Oak was also used, and I have helped tear down old rail fences that sometimes had a few walnut rails. Some chestnut rails still stand at our family farm.

Although life was rugged on a mountain farm, a lot of it was fun and interesting. Maybe the hard working part made it more enjoyable by contrast. We had a feeling of accomplishment just in doing our daily chores, taking care of the animals, feeding then, sheltering them if necessary, and bringing in wood for fuel. Perhaps it's like the hunter who spent the day in the rough, cold mountainous terrain, walking up and down hills, and then coming to a warm cabin with good, hot food. The reward was the hot food, the warm fire, and enjoying each other's company and the many unique visitors.

The views from our farm were spectacular. From our living room we had a view of an uneven valley, wooded,

14

and with a zig zag shape. The last ridge in the distance seemed to look as if it were a dam, cutting off the valley. This was called Bear Wallow Ridge. It seemed strange why this valley did not fill with water, making a huge lake, but it didn't because the creek made a ninety degree turn north at this point.

From the fields on top of the hill we could see forever in almost every direction, and the views were ever changing through the seasons. In the spring the trees would be leafless; then the small blooming trees began to come to life in red and white, with the green ground showing underneath. The other trees would begin to leaf out and grow to full size, and the distant fields would show in a dark, full green in contrast to the yet leafless trees. Parts of these fields would begin to be plowed for the summer crops, showing yet another contrast. After that the freshly planted fields would show green, pointing out further differences in the landscape.

As summer came on, the forests would be completely in green leaves, the crops of grain would ripen and wave in the winds, with the corn fields still green. About this time the oats and wheat would be cradled and tied into sheaves and made into shocks of twelve sheaves. They would look like fields of small golden colored pup tents, both far and near. Later the corn would be cut and made into taller shocks, looking like Indian teepees, while they dried for shucking the ears of corn.

The few acres of buckwheat would be harvested about two months later than the wheat and oats and would be cradled and raked into single sheaves. We would pick up a sheaf just under the dark grain heads, squeezing the sheaf there to hold it together, and then setting it in the stubble to dry. The sheaves would be the same distance apart in even rows, with the black heads of grain looking as if they had necks, which had been formed by our squeezing at that place. Looking at the field from a distance, the sheaves looked like a field of toy soldiers in their black hats standing in drill formation.

From our mountain top fields, all of this could be seen for miles.

During the summer the hay crops were mowed, raked and put into shocks all over the fields to dry before making haystacks. My favorite farm odors were freshly mown hay, freshly turned plowed ground and fertilizer. I have never known another person who liked the smell of fertilizer.

The autumn view from our mountain fields was magnificent. Sometimes it seemed that all of the leaves were in full color at once, as far as the eye could see. The red and golden maples, the yellow poplars, the walnuts, the oaks, and all of the hardwood trees of the Appalachian forests were there. What I saw when hunting along the ridges was beyond description in wild beauty.

Chestnuts, black walnuts, butternuts and hickory nuts could be picked up by the bushels. The nuts from each of these trees seemed to have different flavors, especially chestnuts, and we had to compete with the squirrels and ferry diddles for the chestnuts from certain trees, as they seemed to like the nuts from the same trees we preferred. The best chestnut trees were either in the fields or along the edges of the woods.

Not only were the views ever-changing by season, but sometimes every day. We might have a rainy day, with the fields covered by fog, and we were not able to see anything until the fog lifted. On another day we would be in the mountain fields and see late in the evening the colorful sunset.

There were many things we did when I was young which were done for a few years afterward, but hardly ever now. For example, work sleds were always home made and were also used for travel in the winter. These sleds were made in various ways, especially the sled runners. The runners might be made at a saw mill, maybe twelve to fifteen feet long, with the ends turned up and about four inches thick. They might be made at home of hickory saplings with a natural bend for the turned up end for the front. A sapling might be split to make both runners, or two separate hickory saplings might be used. The sides and bottom would be hewn to make both sides flat. Holes would be bored from the top side about two-thirds of the way through with a hand auger. Most of the old time augers had a hand-made "T" handle on the straight auger. Dowel pins would be whittled from hickory to fit these

[1] A ferry diddle is a small squirrel.

holes, and a top piece would fit on top the same way. Cross braces could be made to strengthen it, and a "bed" built to carry people or equipment. The bed would be made of long, rough boards the length of the sled and probably gotten at a saw mill.

A tongue made of hard wood would be attached to the front, where a double tree would be fastened. Two single trees would be secured to the double tree. The trace chains from the harness could be hooked to the single tree. A breast yoke would be fitted to the front end of the sled tongue and then to the horse collars. Then the horses could pull the sled forward or stop and pull back through the breast yoke, stopping the sled. Soles, or little strips of wood, could be nailed to the bottom of the runners, and were often replaced, thus saving the runners from being quickly worn out. These were used in snow instead of wagons.

One of my earliest memories of a trip in a home made sled was when I must have been three or four years old. Our family went to Grandfather Deitz's house, which was about ten miles away, and I have forgotten about 99% of this trip. Did we start from our home? Did we start from my aunt's house, just a three mile trip? Where did we fill the stone jugs with hot water or heat bricks, which we used, wrapped up, to keep our feet warm? We were all bundled up. I have been told about this, but I don't recall anything about it. Yet I have a completely clear mental snapshot of certain things: the warm jugs or bricks, my father getting out of the sled to open a gate in a farmer's field and crossing a small creek, which might have been about four inches deep. I remember the horses pulling the sled through the water.

Maybe Washington felt the same excitement when he crossed the Delaware.

When we arrived at Grandfather Deitz's house, I clearly remember seeing Grandmother Deitz sitting in the corner smoking a corn cob pipe.

Among the meats we ate and used when company came to eat, chicken was probably number one. We kept a lot of chickens at all times, and especially frying chickens in the summer. It was easy to kill a few and fry them quickly. Mutton was the next most easily available. If a lot of company came for a few days, a young sheep would be

17

butchered and cooked. Wild game was used a lot, mostly in the fall, as all of the boys hunted. The wild meat was mostly squirrel and rabbit.

Beef was not a highly rated meat on the farm as it was difficult to keep a large amount. So usually, when a steer was butchered, it would be divided among a few families until another family butchered a steer.

Mom told of how in earlier days the beef was pickled in salt brine. She described it as tasting terrible. Later they would pull sides of beef into the tree tops on pulleys, and it would be preserved by freezing in the cold winters. It would be lowered with the rope pulley and a portion would be cut off and kept for a while in a cold outbuilding. Pork would be smoked or salted down and kept almost the entire winter.

Our first fruit of the spring season was strawberries, which grew wild in the fields. We never planted strawberries, but if anyone cleared new ground and after a year or two of farming let it lie fallow, the wild strawberries grew almost by the bushel. Usually the near neighbors would also pick strawberries as there were so many the family could not use them all. Mom and the girls canned them as well as blackberries, which grew wild also, and hundreds of gallons were available. The birds ate berries too and planted the seeds without ever reading a book on how and where to plant.

Apples, peaches, pears and plums were planted by the farmers on almost every farm, and the fruits were canned or stored. In July eating apples became available in unlimited varieties. The yellow transparent, strawberry, sweet apples (both red and green, later my favorite), the golden sweet apples were all there. One or another would be ripe at someone's farm, and the eating apples belonged to everyone, not just the owner of the land and the tree, but neighbors, relatives and strangers climbed the fences and got pockets full of apples. Many evenings, after a ten or twelve hour day, I would walk a mile or two to get apples, peaches, etc. I would eat a lot, fill my pockets, hold what I could in my arms and start for home. I don't suppose I ever got home with an uneaten apple or peach due to a country boy's ever hungry, bottomless stomach.

Every two or three years my Father hired a man to trim our fruit trees. This man was considered an expert. We would end up with tons of limbs, which we then cut up and used for firewood. The fruit wood made great, colored flames as it burned. We had one thousand bushels of apples one year in a great variety of apples: the Banana, Northern Spy, Russet, the Black Ben Davis, the Johnson Winters, Rome Beauty, Milam and maybe lots of others that might be cross breeds that would be irreplaceable, except maybe by grafts.

The winter apples would be stored in our cellar. Before the cellar was built, the apples were stored outdoors. Four long, large logs, maybe four feet high, with the sides hewn to one foot thick, formed a pen. Leaves were poured in this pen, then bushels of apples were layered with leaves, and the top was covered to shed the rain. The apples kept well, and usually a bucket of them was in front of the fireplace in the evenings to eat. Family stories say that I could eat a bucket of apples by myself. I really think that my family stretched the truth a bit.

From the time I was about ten I was the only boy still at home old enough to do the outside chores and to furnish the wild game, which was mostly squirrels. I killed the squirrels by hunting along the split rail fences around the fields while going to school and coming home. I would kill a few squirrels on the way to school and hide my gun and the squirrels underneath the school house on a beam away from the younger children. If we had a hired man or hired woman at home, I might send the squirrels home by a passerby. Then I would hunt on the way home. My teachers never minded as long as the gun was unloaded and put away in a safe place.

One evening after school on a rainy evening, my Father called that he had seen a squirrel go up a hickory tree. I got my .22 rifle but couldn't see the squirrel through the thick leaves. I climbed the tree and loaded the rifle, holding to the limb with one hand. Then I shot the squirrel and, as it fell, I caught it with the other hand. Dad asked if I had gotten it. Mumbling answers he couldn't understand, I climbed down far enough to see him and threw the squirrel at him. My grandfather really liked this story.

I think that we had squirrel, squirrel gravy, and biscuits almost every morning for breakfast from early September until Christmas, and I still think these were the world's greatest breakfasts. Mom could make the best gravy I ever tasted. She always said the flavor came from having so many squirrels to cook at one time, and that gave the gravy lots of flavor. Another thing that helped was that I was always hungry from being out in the open cold weather so much.

When I first started squirrel hunting I was nine or ten years old, and the only gun I was allowed to use was an old single shot .22 rifle, which would shoot fairly true, but not where it was aimed. It would always shoot up and to the right. I would then have the challenge of guesswork. I would shoot low and to the left, but I would have to figure out how low and how much to the left, according to how far away the squirrels happened to be. This caused a lot more misses than hits.

An interesting incident happened when some friends of my brother Lawrence asked to hunt. He started to tell them about our woods and how there were good areas and special food trees where there were squirrels and some equally good looking areas with no squirrels. They stopped him, telling him that if squirrels were there, they could find them without help. When Lawrence came home from teaching, they came back without any squirrels. Lawrence insisted that he could get them a few. In about thirty minutes he was back with a supply. Those men were good squirrel hunters--they just didn't know our woods, but it still left them very deflated. After that they took his advice on what areas to hunt.

As I mentioned before, I hunted on the way to and from school, and our other hunting was also hunting on the run as there were so many chores to do. As we went around the farm doing chores, we usually carried a gun so we could shoot squirrels. While we were shucking corn, a dog might tree a squirrel, and we would grab a gun and get one or two squirrels, not missing more than five minutes work. We knew every favorite food tree for the squirrels for a long distance away. When I was in high school I came home one Saturday to help in the fields, and our brother-in-law came with me to hunt. Throughout the day he would come by where I was working, and I would stop for a few minutes, go to the top of one of the hills, and point out a tree with a squirrel feeding. The tree might be a quarter of a mile away. Later he told another brother-in-law that I was spotting squirrels farther than he could spot a cow. Until then I didn't realize he didn't know what I was seeing. I was merely looking for a favorite food tree and seeing the limbs and leaves moving when a squirrel jumped from one limb to another, which was easy to see.

I have always thought of this incident when someone seemed to be an expert on something. Maybe he was only doing something simple.

For organized entertainment we had pie socials, the last day of school, children's day at church, and a 4th of July picnic. In school we had spelling bees and what we called geography races.

Children's Day was at the church, and there was a picnic, with the children saying their "pieces," which were recitation and memorized poetry. When I was a younger child I was involved in reciting poetry and other things. If I reminded anyone in any way of Patrick Henry, it was never mentioned. The rest of the day was spent at the picnic tables, visiting and maybe listening to a welcoming speech by someone.

On the 4th of July there was a picnic with games, foot races and jumping matches. Sometimes we met at the Amick farm to pick service berries, which usually grew on small bushes or small trees. On this farm there were large service trees (we called them sarvice trees), which were as large as cherry trees. Picnickers used to hold sheets under the trees and shake the full limbs above them and get gallons of the berries.

The "sarvice" berries resembled wild tea berries and were very tasty. We had lots of wild teaberries at that time. One of my favorite plants was penny royal, which grew everywhere in our country, and I would pull it up green and make tea late in the evening. It is still my all-time favorite tea, although I can't find any now, not even among the herb teas. We could find gingseng to sell, but we didn't have wild ramps in our area.

As I remember the sounds, the odors, the views and tastes, everything seemed stronger and made a much greater impression on my senses than now. There was so much more time to see, smell, hear and taste. Even though chores, work and school kept a person busy, we were moving slower by walking, riding or driving horses, so we just didn't go flying by everything.

Among these vivid memories were the sounds. There

was a lumber mill two or three miles away (as the crow flies), and we could hear the work whistle most of the time, especially on a still day. Sometimes, late in the evening, nearly dusk, the whole world was quiet except for the lowing of the cattle and the bleating of the sheep. Then might come the eerie, mournful sound of a train whistle through the valley and the hills, The mournful whistle sounded as if it came from far, far away and long, long ago. The sun was still on the hill top, but the valleys were blue, and into this came the wailing sound, as if this sound had been echoing from the very first train whistle that ever sounded in that country and had been echoing in the hills and valleys ever since. It just had to be the saddest lament in the world. Even though I knew exactly what and where it was, it still seemed to be coming from a hundred miles away and a hundred years ago.

When it got darker, the stars or moon seemed to be much closer and brighter. The main difference was that we actually stopped and really saw them. We just didn't glance at them as we hurried into the house.

Another favorite memory has been country roads. During dry summers it was my job to take our work horses up the road to near my grandfather's house to water them, both at noon and evening. This road went through the woods all the way, and there would be a unique mixture of shadows and sun on the road. The leaves would blow gently, changing the shapes of the shadows.

We always had names for the various spots along the road, as though they were streets. There was the black stump, the half-way place (half-way between our house and Granddad's), the flying squirrel tree where flying squirrels lived for several years, the rocky hollow (Uncle Owen's road, a side road to my uncle's house), and the sulphur spring where I watered the horses. This spring never ran dry.

Our farm dog would also make the trip, chasing wild animals and always treeing a squirrel or two.

Another memory is of the bullbats[3], or that was our name for them. These birds would fly out late in the evening by the thousands, catching bugs in the air and

[1] According to Webster, a bullbat is a night hawk, any of a group of birds related to the whippoorwill, with brown mottled feathers and broad deeply cleft bill.

flying from ground level to about half a mile above Hickory Flats Ridge for a distance of at least seven miles. The air would be filled with them. I used to stand in the yard and try to hit one with a broomstick, probably swinging every few seconds they were so thick, but I never hit one. Where they went in the day time I never knew, as I never saw one during the day. We didn't have that many cliffs or caves in that area for them to hide in. Whatever happened to them, I have no idea, and I haven't seen them in years in that country.

BOYHOOD SCHOOL DAYS
By Dennis Deitz

My first teacher, Charley Williams, a single man at that time, is still living (1982), and is the father of eight children. I remember that he had a stiff knee, but he could run fairly fast and play games with the children. He was considered a good teacher, although it is hard for me to remember that much about him. I only remember my second grade teacher who would take his hands to straighten my head back to a forward position. I guess I had trouble keeping my head on straight. My mother and my father were probably my teachers three or four terms in my eight grades in one room country schools, and I had another teacher who was a relative and who also was a good teacher. One of my men teachers had just been married the summer before, and now it seems that most of that term was spent with him on his honeymoon the summer before. At that time I thought we must have heard every little detail, but now I'm sure he left out a lot.

Overall, I was blessed with a lot of special teachers. Their ability to control us, and not to the tune of a hickory stick, was unbelievable. It was great to sit and listen to the upper grades recite history, geography and arithmetic. If a person was interested as I was in these subjects, it was wonderful how much could be learned by the third or fourth grade.

We lived for the fifteen minutes of recess in the mornings and afternoons, as well as the hour for lunch. We spent these minutes on almost a dead run, playing games, such as Andy Over, but the proper name may have been Ante Over. We threw a ball over the school house, and a member of the team on the other side of the house caught it, and the team on that side would run around the house and try to hit someone with the ball before the other team made it safely to the other side. One arm was held behind you so the opposing team would not know who had the ball. If you were hit, you were out for that game. This continued until only one person was left, and his side won.

We played prisoner's base, blackman's base, shoot the buck, plain base, fox and goose in the snow, and fox and

24

hounds. In fox and hounds, half of the children were the hounds, and they chased the foxes. As each fox was touched, he was out until every fox was caught. The last few foxes were greatly out-numbered. Then the foxes became hounds, and the other side tried to catch the foxes sooner than the first group.

This was a rugged game in our country because of the rough ground. We would run over large rocks and jump into briers and brambles to escape. Some of the teams would have six year old girls on them, and they would get bumps, bruises and skinned knees, but they accepted this, and I don't remember them crying over the rough play.

There was a steep hillside field near our school, and when the snow crusted over several inches deep, we would take old school desk tops and slide down this long, steep hill on the desk tops. Sometimes the tops would hit a stump which was sticking above the snow, and we would go flying through the air and on to the bottom of the hill. We might hit another stump on the way down. Again, I don't remember the young girls making much of a fuss about a spill. At no time did the girls ask for mercy or special treatment.

Many of our schoolmates stayed all night with us, along with pupils of our parents when they taught at nearby schools. We had great fun playing games like blind man's bluff, hide and seek and other games in our big upstairs rooms at night. Our parents were not bothered nor worried by the loud rackets we made. They might even join in the games. The girls made batches of pop corn or candy, taffy for pulling or maybe caramel popcorn balls. These children, now grandparents, still mention to us these things as highlights of their lives and speak with great affection for my parents.

Before dark and before the fun started, our chores had to be done, and visitors helped with these. This was also part of fun on the run. I had a great feeling of accomplishment from the work, for I knew I was a valuable cog in being able to eat and stay warm. Being needed was great satisfaction, I think. I may have been of the last generation of children who ever got this feeling.

A one room school was a great experience. If you had good teachers, and you could remember at all, you just had to learn basics. Most of my brothers and sisters were

25

really good students. I wasn't that good, but I did have advantages since both my parents were teachers. They and the older children saw to it that I did my assignments, and I had other exceptionally good teachers. One natural advantage was that I always liked history, and I could listen to the classes for the older pupils. It was like story telling to me. During geography classes I would fantasize about exciting, faraway places.

On Fridays we would have contests to see which one could locate names of cities on maps. Arithmetic was like a puzzle to be solved, but spelling came the hard way, with drills and a push at home. Writing was a disaster. I had teachers in grammar and English who would pound those subjects into my head, no matter how hard I tried to keep them out. I still believe that by the third or fourth grade I could have passed an eighth grade test in history or geography. I think I still remember ninety percent of what I learned in the one room schools and have forgotten more than ninety percent of what I learned in high school and college.

Sometimes, late in the fall, when there were fewer chores, a schoolmate and I could hunt or trap. These schoolmates were great fun and likeable, and the ones who are still living are still like that today.

When I was fifteen I stayed with my sister and went to the ninth grade to junior high school. This was the first time I had ever been among strangers, and it took a little while to get close to them as they were friends already, and I was an outsider. One little incident really got me in with a group of boys. Two or three months after I started to school, I was walking home with some of the boys from a little town a couple of miles away when one of them suggested that we hide behind a mound and snowball the group from where I was living. After ten or fifteen minutes of snowballing, it seemed to me that snowballs were hitting me from every direction, and I began to look for my cohorts. I spotted the last of them in flight a quarter of a mile away in retreat. I was doing battle all alone with about thirty boys. This group, from then on, considered me the bravest of the brave for doing battle all alone. I never explained that I was doing battle through ignorance, not bravery.

The next three years I stayed with Aunt Rosa, who was

keeping a boarding house now, and I rode a school bus about ten miles to high school. Again I was on the outside of a close knit group, but this time it was easier as about half the students rode school buses and were also outsiders. The last two years I played football and hitchhiked back to my aunt's house in the evening. This helped me to get to know more of the students better. These people were never really strangers, just new friends. They were a fun loving group, and, along with them, I probably stayed on the brink of falling into trouble. How I ever escaped being called on the carpet I'll never know.

Most of my teachers were pretty tolerant of our pranks as long as they weren't too noisy or disruptive. Once I had a good, serious man teacher who liked a good laugh. Although he didn't teach English, he would get upset about our compositions. One day he gave us a composition assignment and said he was not going to tolerate missed punctuation marks and warned us that he was going to take off ten percent of every punctuation mark we missed. The next day I turned in my composition without putting in even one punctuation mark. I did add an extra page full of punctuation marks, with a postscript saying USE WHERE NEEDED. He accepted it, saying, technically, he supposed I had followed instructions. He told everyone what I had done, and he considered it a great joke.

Another time I barely missed getting into trouble. Our old maid English teacher didn't have a sense of humor and was not very tolerant. One day she had us reading dry English literature from a large text book. The passages were numbered, and she was calling for us to read aloud by calling our names. It was pretty dull, as it took about ten minutes to read about someone going up the stairs, so I got an old Zane Gray western out of my desk, placed it in front of my text book and started reading. The hero was in deep trouble, surrounded by outlaws, and I was really absorbed in getting him out. According to my classmates, the teacher started watching my interest in this dull material. It just wasn't natural. As someone finished his assignment, she called my name. Just as she called my name, a girl behind me whispered the next number. I dropped my hero, who was in deep trouble and, as it happened, I was looking at the number the classmate had

27

whispered, and I read on without a hitch. The class roared. The teacher's view was blocked, so she could only guess what had happened. Again I came out of a bad situation by the skin of my teeth.

One of my teachers nearing ninety years old always reminded me of an answer I gave her in Civics class. She asked, "Why do people try to keep their farms clean and their houses painted?" My answer was, "To make their neighbors jealous." She always said this was her favorite all-time answer in her teaching career.

After graduating from high school I went to Glenville State Teachers' College and stayed there until the depression took its toll, and my mother lost her teaching job. She had always taught on a renewable teacher's certificate, and she didn't teach again until the war changed the abundant supply of teachers to a shortage.

Glenville was an excellent place to go to school. No one had any money, so we had to make our own entertainment, which was a lot more fun than paid entertainment. While I was there I made a friend in Eddie Rohrbaugh, who was my boxing coach and had married my first cousin. He was the son of the president of the college, and he spent many hours in my room, telling stories about the earlier days at Glenville, always pacing up and down in the room while he talked. Last winter I wrote to him and asked him for some of these stories, but he only remembered what will be included later.

Eddie took me to a golden gloves boxing tournament in Clarksburg, WV, where I won. When I returned to school after the tournament, I didn't have any marks on me, so the boys stripped me to the waist and still couldn't find any marks or bruises. Then they made up stories about what had happened. One story was that I had hired a professional to box under my name. Another was that I had talked to a sportswriter and got him to make up a story, with me as the hero and winner, and printing it on the sports page. They said that since there were no marks, there had been no fight, and that I had even scored a phantom knockout.

SCHOOL REUNIONS

We had a close knit class at Rainelle High School and held reunions every five years for many years. Following is a talk I gave at one of the reunions. Last summer when I was drafted to be Master of Ceremonies, I used this opportunity to tease some of my old classmates and class sponsor.

Five years ago when we had our last reunion, Fred invited each of us to say a few words about ourselves. At that time I was not prepared for the opportunity since in my case it takes a little time and imagination to come up with something flattering. This time, however, I am prepared.

When I asked Fred for a little extra time to say my piece, he attempted to discourage the idea in his own tactful way. As I recall, his exact words were: "You know, back on the farm I always vowed I'd rather die than hoe corn; but I swan, I do believe I'd rather hoe corn than listen to you talk."

But, as you can see, persistence finally paid off.

Seriously, rather than talk about myself, I wanted to add a footnote about the rather remarkable character of our class of 1932 and how it gives the lie to a popular social theory today.

In my opinion, our class is a living rebuttal to the modern argument that crime and juvenile delinquency are the fruit of poverty and disadvantage.

If ever a group of youngsters was acquainted with hardship, adversity, and disadvantage, we were. We grew up in the heart of Appalachia and graduated in the midst of the great depression. At the time our middle class working parents were at the nadir of their economic fortunes--or perhaps I should say, misfortunes. I doubt if their average income exceeded $500 per year. And if that was bad, their usually large families made it worse economically. As you remember, when we graduated there were no jobs waiting, and there was no money for college. Compounding this disadvantage, there were no scholarships available, even for our top students. If that wasn't poverty and lack of opportunity, I'm afraid I'm miserably misinformed.

Presumably such conditions are supposed to breed delinquents and criminals, bums and reliefers. If so, our class missed its date with destiny. The fact is, allowing for some doubt in the case of myself, you all turned out to be fairly respectable people. The record shows that you started out in well–below average circumstances and have climbed to well-above average conditions. We have these records for you. We have made our own way. We have raised and educated fine children, and a few of our number have risen to considerable distinction. And what is even more remarkable, I personally do not know of a single member of this disadvantaged class who has ever been in serious trouble or has spent a night in jail. (Please don't confess--it might spoil everything.)

Since there does indeed seen to be some sort of relationship between poverty and bad character today, how do we explain the character of our disadvantaged class of yesterday? My personal theory is that we had then some advantages missing in the lives of the modern poor that money simply can't buy. I'd like to cite a few.

For one thing, we were probably the last graduating class this country will ever see (that was) not told that the world owed us a living. We were a little dumb about this idea, fortunately. As a result we pulled ourselves up by our own bootstraps to the point where we are carrying our modern disadvantaged counterparts on our economic shoulders with our considerable taxes.

But undoubtedly our chief advantage was our parents. They gave us those things parents are for, those things so obviously missing today--good, solid, no-nonsense discipline and supervision. Had you mentioned 'child psychology' to them, they might have thought you were talking about a new adolescent disease, probably thinking that they could bring it out the same as measles with sheep manure tea and cure it with wild yeller root or sulphur and molasses.

Another thing, too. They didn't allow us much room to get lost in that gray area between black and white. They brooked no fine academic distinction between right and wrong. When it came to good and bad, their trumpet never gave us an uncertain sound. And they were willing to enforce their convictions with whatever measures were necessary.

Knowing this, very little force was required. They firmly believed one could not be partially truthful or half honest any more than one could be half pregnant. For them right was right and wrong was wrong. And if something wasn't right, then it was wrong.

These things I believe largely account for the difference between our disadvantaged class and our contemporary counterparts. And that difference makes me quite proud to be a member of the class of 1932.

Perhaps the Rev. Westlake has summed it up best with this comment:

"It would naturally follow that children from this type of parents would have a class motto which says, 'Build for character and not for fame.' "

We have gathered here for this reunion from far and near, and I hope you are glad you came. It is wonderful to see old friends again, and I miss those who couldn't make it this year.

I will start this off by making a personal report on the last five years. Several things have changed in the family. We have a new grandson and a new great grandson. We have lost a couple of family members, including my mother who made it to almost 101 years. My wife, Madeline, had a heart attack this year, but she has recovered nicely. One of her biggest problems was surviving my cooking for a couple of months, although she was finally convinced that I worshipped her as I kept bringing her burnt offerings.

Now to get back to our high school memories. Mrs. Manion was not only our sponsor, but also our history teacher. As sponsor, she looked after us with love and understanding. How she could love us was beyond our parents, and how she could understand us was beyond their understanding. She was a good history teacher and a loyal southerner. I want you to know, Mrs. Manion, that we all know that the South did win the Civil War. When some of us went on to college and read the northern propaganda about the North winning the war, we always put a footnote at the bottom of our test papers, saying, according to this textbook.

For the first few months her southern accent caused problems in history class. The only thing that saved us was that neither could she understand our hillbilly accent. We did have a communication problem.

I remember once that she asked a question that must have gone something like this. "When the fo'mah Thomas Jackson stood on the hill above Bull Run like a stonewall, why did the wah go on so much longer?"

Most of us were completely baffled. We not only didn't know the answer, we didn't even know the question. Finally one of our farm boys bailed us out as he seemed to catch on to the southern accent quicker than most of us. He said he did know a farmer named Thomas Jackson, that he did remember when his cattle broke loose from the knob field, and the bull ran off and had jumped over the stone wall and escaped. He didn't remember that the bull was gone that much longer when they finally caught him.

We are glad to have Wilbur Gladwell and his wife, Janet, with us. Wilbur retired not long ago, after forty years with Carbide in the Kanawha Valley. Someone asked Wilbur if he was moving back to Greenbrier County, and he said, "Oh, no! Can you believe that in those mountains you can't even see what you are breathing?"

Dennis Hume and his wife are here too. I remember Dennis as a good student when he was awake. He was good in math except for percentages--he just couldn't master percentages. Later he went into the building business and could cipher with anyone, but, even after high school, he had trouble with percentages. I remember seeing him dressed real sharp, driving around in a shiny car, with the top down and his hair blowing away in the wind, when most of us didn't have two nickles to rub together. I finally got him stopped long enough to ask him about his apparent prosperity. He told me that he had that territory to sell a gadget that he was able to buy for a dollar and sell for three dollars. He said, "You would be amazed at the money you can make at three percent."

Carter Marks is here too. Carter was one of the best football players we ever had who played on a broken leg. That would have handicapped most of us, Carter.

I'm glad to see Everett Puckett, our class valedictorian, who in those days was a quiet, serious, friendly person,

32

well liked by everyone. Then the word got around that he not only carried his books home at night, but he actually studied them. We sort of thought of him as being a little strange after that.

Laird Wall moved to the other end of the county, and I haven't seen him often, but I remember him with pleasure.

Audrey Reynolds Selby and I have ancestors in common, I have found out from my research in genealogy. We want to thank these ancestors who worked with a passion to make us your classmates.

Alma Weatherford Bennett Barnard was way ahead of the times with Women's Lib. I can still hear her saying, "I don't know why they won't let girls play football. I might not be able to tackle very well, but I'll bet I could cause a lot of holding penalties." We're glad you are here, Alma.

Next is Lou Williams Reed and her husband, Bruce. I will mention Lou again, but I want to tell you about Bruce, whom I have known almost as long as the rest of you. Several years ago I ran into Bruce, and he told me that he thought about divorcing Lou. I asked him why. I said Lou is one of the nicest persons I ever knew. Bruce said, "Oh, I know that, but it's money. She is always saying, "Give me five dollars, give me ten dollars, give me twenty dollars.'

When I asked what in the world she was doing with all that money, he said, "How could I know? I haven't given her any yet."

I want to give you a puzzle about Mary Williams Tamplin, Lou and their sister, Jesse. This is true, not that I haven't been telling the truth up to now, but I may have added a little truth to the facts sometimes. Sometime during 1982 each of these sisters will be 67 years old--no twins or triplets. When you figure that out, take this one on. The first wedding they ever attended was when their grandfather and grandmother were married.

I remember Mary Lefler Wiseman as a student who asked questions. They say that this was always true. In fact, it started on her first day in school in the first grade. When the teacher was explaining the rules, she told the first graders, "If any of you need to go to the bathroom, just hold up your hand." Mary looked real puzzled and asked her first question: "How would that help?"

Ralph Judy like the rest of us, is getting older. A few months ago he began to worry that his love life wasn't what it once was, so he went to this young doctor who was gung ho on computers. He thought he could solve all medical problems on the computer. After Ralph told him his concerns, the doctor fed all of the information into the computer, such as weight, height, age, etc. He then told Ralph he wanted him to run exactly 14 miles a day for 10 days and call him. Ten days later Ralph called back explaining how he had followed instructions, etc.

The doctor said, "How about you love life? Did it help that?" Ralph impatiently answered, "How the devil would I know? I'm 140 miles from home."

Lola Callison Westlake is here tonight, and she, Fred, Captola and Woody have been key people in making this reunion a success. She has been the essential person, like you find in every successful organization, who has done all the correspondence and organization, while someone like me stands up here and talks.

There is a story I heard about Lola a long time ago, and I want to share it with you. One time when she was in grade school, she changed schools. Her new teacher talked with her and filled out the information chart concerning her age, address, sex, parents' names, and all those other statistics that schools seem to want to know. She told Lola to take it home and have her parents to check it for errors. Lola took it home, gave it to her parents and announced, "I don't like that new teacher. Look there, she gave me an F in sex, and we haven't even had one lesson in it yet."

Are you interested in the answers to those puzzles I gave you earlier about Jessie, Mary and Lou? Well, Jessie, the oldest, turned 68 in February 1982; Mary, the middle one turned 67 in Jan. 1982; and Lou will turn 67 in November 1982.

Their Grandfather Nutter married their Grandmother Williams, and that was the first wedding they ever attended.

OUR TELEPHONE CENTRAL

My Mother told of the first telephones in our country in 1913, the year I was born. Our house was used for the telephone central and had five trunk lines. She was teaching at that time, and she would open the Central when she arose in the morning about five o'clock, keep it open until eight, then close it until she came home at four in the afternoon and keep it open until bed time. Pretty soon most of us could operate it, even at a very young age. I mentioned in another chapter about the first time Dad came in and saw my six year old sister, standing on a chair and acting as the telephone operator. He walked in the kitchen, scratching his head, and asked, "Betty, does that little rascal know what she is doing?"

As all of us grew old enough to stand on a chair, we became telephone operators, postal workers, or whatever. We never became the type of post masters as did the post master in town in later years. This post master was noted for reading open post cards. One time my nephew wrote his mother a card, and in the middle of the card he wrote, "John, if you see my Mother pass, please give her this card." John watched carefully for the mother, stopped her and delivered the card.

I remember those telephone trunk lines leading into the house. The last section of the lines was run from the pole and hooked to the insulators on the porch. They were uninsulated lines, with the lines having a short bend to hook to rings on the insulators on the porch. When a lightning storm was seen coming, one of us would run to the porch, stand on the bannister, unhook all of the trunk lines, and let them drop to the ground. We would later watch lightning run through the lines and ground into the yard. If the lines touched, the lightning might run back through another trunk line. We tried to keep them apart, but we enjoyed the excitement.

During heavy snows and sleet, limbs would break off, fall on the lines along the road and break them.

I am not sure how our telephone system was financed or how costs of upkeep were handled. From what I can remember and can gather from family memories, it was apparently a form of co-op. The poles were cut and put up by the poeple who put in telephones. The telephones could have been bought through Sears Roebuck. They were battery operated. People who had telephones may not have paid a regular fee.

Mr. Marvin Haynes, now of Dunbar, but who lived in that country many years ago, told me that he helped with the poles and lines and ordered his telephone from Sears and paid for it. He doesn't remember who paid for the glass insulators and the lines, but he assumes the co-op members split these costs. Members also took care of the upkeep without pay, and our family thinks that we maintained the central without charge. The whole system was run by batteries as there was no electric.

Repair of the Central was done on the "By-golly and by-gosh" system. My older brother remembers that in that country there were no mechanics or electricians as no one had engines or electricity. If the telephone central broke down, a neighbor would be called in. He was a member of the co-op, and by some strange reasoning, my father would proclaim him an expert. Dad probably thought he was an expert because he didn't do anything else much. This man would usually fail, and my twelve year old brother would climb up the telephone operator's chair and reconnect the proper wires to match each other. He never figured why it had to be rewired, but he thinks now that when the lead in wires were disconnected before a lightning storm they were re-hooked wrong. He now wonders why he didn't think of that then.

Everyone listened in on the party lines, even though it wasn't their ring signal. Most country people were hungry for news and company. Too, this was a good way to spread news of the need for help.

Some of the young fellows tried to use the party line to have fun by calling a friend and tell a ridiculous story to see if some eavesdropper would believe it, especially some of the older women whose hard working, child bearing lives had left them so serious. Usually their voices would be recognized, and a member of her family would tell the mother not to believe the jokester. A friend of mine really thought he had achieved success when he called a cousin and described a bad forest fire during a deep winter snowstorm. Later an old grandmother called him back for more details.

OUR KNOB FIELD

The expression "knob field" may not be familiar to all readers, but people who grew up in the mountains probably will understand. A knob field was a high round hill, rather than a ridge. If the land was not too steep and could be cultivated because of the gentle slopes, it would be called a knob field. Sometimes one of these fields could be plowed with a turn plow by going completely around and around from the bottom to the top, continuously. This way, stopping at each of the four corners of a flat field was avoided, and the plow would not have to be pulled back to start down the next side. This required strength.

My first plowing experience was plowing my grandfather's knob field, as it was much easier. When I was about thirteen or fourteen, I plowed this field, starting at the bottom and going around and around, never having to back up the plow to make the ninety degree turn required in a flat field. This field was fairly rock free, and this caused me to get a little careless. Usually, when plowing a rocky field, you would keep your hands firmly on the plow handles and your body far enough back to be in the clear of the handles in case you suddenly hit a rock under the surface, which might cause the plow handles to hit you.

One day I was plowing this near knob field with my body between the plow handles when I hit a large rock, jerking the handles from my hands, and allowing the handles to hit my ribs. Down I went, with the air knocked out of me. With my breath gone I could not yell, "whoa" to the team, so I had to run after the plow and stop the horses. I must have looked like a drunk chasing a bottle.

One of our neighbors once plowed a large knob field like this and then laid off or furrowed for corn in the same manner, thus having only one row of corn for eight acres.

My brother, Granville, with his great imagination, used

to tell of a neighbor who had a knob field planted in corn. When he cultivated this corn when it got up pretty high, he had to cultivate the corn all the way to the top of the knob hill and couldn't get the horse out without tearing up some of the corn, so he had to follow the same row all of the way back to the bottom, still cultivating all of the way to the bottom.

Granville always said the neighbor spent three days and nights getting all of the way to the top and back. When someone questioned his version, he would always say, "I can show you the proof. I will show you the knob hill where it happened." This was Granville's method of proving his wild stories: "I will show you exactly where it happened."

If people did not know what to expect from Granville and didn't analyze what he had said, they would be inclined to think why would any reasonable man want any more logical proof. Granville would speak in a very positive, serious, logical tone, and he loved it when someone failed to think his story through.

FAMILY

STEVE HARRISON

Emerson and Watson Deitz, circa 1880

MY FATHER, WATSON DEITZ

My father, an identical twin to Emerson Deitz, was a school teacher as far back as the early 1890's and was teaching at the time of his death in 1928. During his life he was also a surveyor, a merchant, and a farmer. He and his twin were widely known in Nicholas, Greenbrier and Fayette Counties, West Virginia. His twin brother, Emerson, was usually listed among the prominent people in West Virginia in the 1920's.

Dad ran for County Clerk in 1920 and, although living at

the very western end of the county and the least populated part, he was only beaten by a few hundred votes. The man who beat him held the position for about 40 years and always remained a good friend to my father. Dad was always proud that he only lost three votes in his home precinct out of 150 votes. He lost two of them because a married couple felt he should have hired a car to take them to the polling place. One man told Dad that he crossed his ticket to vote for him for the first time in his eighty odd years.

The twins, Watson and Emerson, were from childhood mischievous. They loved to play jokes and pranks on each other and everyone else too. Their father enjoyed their pranks and was an easy going person who didn't do much to curb their activities. Six adoring sisters believed the twins to be the best, the smartest, and the wittiest people anywhere, and they would tell anyone who would listen. The twins were opposite to their father in temperament. They both had what might be called gun powder tempers, for they would blow up in a flash, but the anger was over just as quickly. Dad hardly ever blew up at anyone--just at things, and he would say some uproariously funny things on these occasions.

His father lived on a farm that had a barn perched on the side of a hill. The upper part or hay mows were level with the hill behind it. He would put a platform to the hill behind the barn so that hay could be stored in the mow (loft) from a level position. On one occasion a cow walked across the platform and into the hay mow. The floor in the hay mow was loose fence rails, causing the cow's legs to slip between the rails, and the cow became stranded. My father, just a boy, found her and tried to drive her out. This was impossible without some mechanical lifting help. His father came by and saw the predicament and, in his unexcitable way said, "Watson, you are very good at handling a cow on the ground, but you don't know a thing in the world about handling a cow in a hay mow."

Above this hillside was a flat field where they had a field full of corn and pumpkins. My grandfather had followed a path around the hillside when he went to work. The twins were ten or twelve years old, and they spent several hours rolling pumpkins to the brink of the hill. When their father returned along this hillside path, they started rolling

40

pumpkins at him. After a long acrobatic dance, dodging the pumpkin attack, he made his way to the house. In keeping with his nature, he treated it as a great joke.

The twins taught, worked, farmed and took care of their parents and had so much enjoyment out of their jokes, tricks and country debates that they remained bachelors until they were thirty years old. They were so identical that no one could tell them apart, not even their sisters.

It was written in a Sunday Charleston paper thirty years after Dad's death that a Nicholas County legend was told that the Deitz twins were so identical that when one took a laxative he never had to tell the other one as it would work for him too.

They used their identical looks as a great source for amusement, fun and tricks. They loved to see someone who had been talking to the other twin previously and try to continue the last conversation which had been had, and see if the discussion could be continued without the person realizing he was talking with the other twin.

A favorite trick was to go to see the other's girl friend and see if they could keep her from catching on that this was the wrong twin. The girl might start discussing where they had been together, who they had talked with and what had been said. They accepted this as a great mental challenge, and almost a character study of all of their acquaintances. When the girl might ask what someone had answered to a certain question or statement, they got so that either of them could say almost exactly what that person's response would have been. Although sometimes they were caught or told of doing this, some of these bright country girls would suspect that they might try this sort of thing and try to trap them into a confession. The girl might ask about someone they had seen while they were together or what had been said. It was up to the twin who was there to know whether the incident was fact or fiction, try to figure it out and squirm out of a direct answer.

Even after they were both married and separated several years, my father would go to Richwood and might meet a friend of his twin. This person would call him Emerson and start a conversation. Dad would accept this as a challenge and see if he could get by pretending to be Emerson. He might not know the man's name or occupation. Sometimes he could get enough information in

41

conversation to know this person by reputation through his twin to get by easily. Sometimes he had to get by blindly and usually succeeded. Dad then might set a trap for Emerson by telling this person of a paper or magazine exactly fitting to the subject of the conversation and that he would bring it to the store or post office the next day and have the person promise to stop to get it.

When the person would stop and ask Uncle Emerson about it, he would immediately know what had happened. Uncle Emerson would accept the challenge to see if he could figure out what the person was talking about and might actually produce the item involved. The twins didn't consider the third party as being involved as much as trying to get ahead of the other twin.

Dad's favorite joke on his twin was when Uncle Emerson had saddled up a beautiful saddle horse they owned and had gone to church with a girl friend, tying the horse up outside the church (where else?) Dad then saddled up the most scroungy horse on the farm, went to this church, exchanged horses and rode on to see his girl friend.

Dad always regretted that he never had a picture of Uncle Emerson's face when he came outside after service and saw his new riding horse.

My father and his twin were very athletic. Old friends from their boyhood days used to tell me that Emerson could lay a stick on dad's head, back up just one step and jump over the stick while they held it level at that height. I was only 14 when my Dad died, and he was in his late fifties, so I don't remember seeing him jump that high, but I do remember seeing him out-jump everyone at a Fourth of July picnic attended by about two hundred people.

I do remember him having me try to hit him with a rubber ball from a distance of no more than ten or twelve fet. This was an old time type of contest, and it was unbelievable how close you could throw from and have someone dodge the ball. Dad always said he had trouble dodging a left-handed person consistently as it was harder to react against a new angle.

My Father was a warm, generous, well liked person by neighbors, acquaintances, and especially by his students, nieces and nephews. His quick, high temper caused him to say really funny things when he was mad, but in no way meaning to be funny. I don't remember too many incidents as I was younger and didn't know him as long as the older members of the family. Granville, the oldest child, of course, being the story teller, remembered the funny incidents. He told of the time that Dad made paths going to all the out buildings during a deep snow. He had gone to the barn and let the horses out to go to the watering trough. All of them came back but a horse called Charley. Dad called and called, and still Charley didn't come to the barn. Dad hadn't put his boots on because of the path to the barn, so he had to wade through the deep snow, get Charlie by the halter and lead him back to the barn. By this time Dad was mad. He jerked on Charley's halter, slapped him with his open hand and said, "Now the next time I call, you answer."

Another time a sleet hit the farm, the winds blew and two or three sections of worm rail fence slid down the hill. Dad laid these sections back, but before he could anchor them, being ice covered, they slid over the hill again. He went through this about two more times before he got them anchored. He then looked heavenward, still mad, and said, "Now let's see who's the best man."

Granville, my oldest brother, told about the time he had gone above the road to milk. Mom had rearranged the furniture, putting the mirror of a dresser in line with the front window. Dad always kept a big fire in the fireplace. After milking and while holding a bucket of milk in each hand, he turned and saw fire reflecting through the mirror. Thinking that the house was on fire, he cleared both fences, still holding a bucket in each hand, ran to the house, opened the front door and saw the answer. Granville's story was that Dad threw a fit because the house wasn't on fire.

Another story Granville told was about a time when Dad owned a mean buck sheep who would really butt if you crossed his pasture field. Granville had hit him with a club and was never bothered again by that sheep. Dad didn't know about this, so one day they went out to work in the fields, and Granville purposely climbed the fence and took a short cut. Dad looked dubious, but seeing a fourteen year old who wasn't afraid, he followed and really got butted by the buck sheep.

Mother and Dad kept the post office and had the telephone central at our house from before the time I could remember. Our Mother always thought that any of the children could handle any job that came up, almost as soon as they could walk or, at least, when they could read. This included taking care of the telephone central or doing the post office work.

I stayed with my sister and her husband and went to junior high school. The following summer the Principal, Mr. Stalnaker, came by our house and stopped in. Only my youngest sister and I were there. He asked for a tour of our farm house, and I showed him around. During this time the mail arrived (by horseback), and when we got to the room where the mail was kept and sorted, there sat my little ten year old sister, who actually looked about five, sorting the mail. She had the mail bags across her lap, each end on the floor, as they were made to fit across a horse behind the saddle. Her feet were several inches off the floor, and she was sorting and re-routing mail like a veteran. The look on Mr. Stalnaker's face was plainly asking, "What in the world is going on with Uncle Sam's mail?" I didn't even try to explain.

I used to be fairly close to some of my older first cousins who used to visit back and forth with my family. They loved to tell me stories or funny incidents about Dad-- things that had happened when I was too young to remember. Since I know Dad was among their all time favorite persons, I like to hear the stories. Dad's nephew, Cecil, told how the whole family traveled a few miles by wagon to visit for a weekend, and Dad would play games with them. Cecil had never seen Dad's temper. They started playing some game with about fifteen children involved. About this time a hog broke out through a wire fence and cut itself badly. Dad blew up at the incident. In a second every child disappeared completely, like a covey of quail sighting a fox.

Dad doctored the hog, put him back in the field and repaired the fence while the nieces and nephews watched, peering from their hiding places. Then Dad started beckoning with an arm, saying "Come on, come on, don't you want to finish the game?"

I met an older neighbor boy a few years ago in Charleston who started talking about Dad. He said that when he was 10 or 12 he used to walk through the woods by a near cut to come to our place for the mail. His family always asked if he had seen Dad lose his temper, and he said, "no." He thought Dad was the greatest, friendliest person alive, a person who would always talk with him, One day he came for the mail and Dad was taking a shoe off the horse. Charlie. The horse kicked him. Dad totally blew up, and Lundy said it almost scared him to death.

Dad taught many terms of school, and many of his former students referred to him as their all-time favorite teacher. One girl, who is yet a close friend to our family, tells of having him for a teacher when he rode a horse about two miles to the school. She was a small girl and walked about the same distance to the school, through the fields and woods with her older brother and cousins. If a big snow fell during the day, he would say to her, "Those long-legged boys can make it through the snow, but I don't want a little girl to try it." Then he would put her on the horse behind him and bring her home for the night and take her back to school the next day. She still says, "I will remember him until the day I die."

Mother always said that if the president of the United States was eating at one end of the dinner table and the biggest bum in the country was at the other end, and you could only see Dad in the middle. You would never know by watching Dad which one was sitting at which end of the table.

Dad couldn't turn anyone down who told him a hard luck story, even if it took his last dollar, and even if he knew it would never be paid back. In case of a loan, he would have a note signed, sometimes for unreliable people. This led to great problems for Mom, as the depression started soon after his death, and some of us were still young. Every passerby and visitor to the postoffice was invited in to eat, causing lots of cooking at our house.

At his death in 1928 so many friends attended the funeral services it was necessary to hold the services outside, although they were held at a fairly large country church. Four ministers who had known him most of their lives spoke. He is buried at Sugar Grove, Nicholas County, within a mile of Nutterville, WV.

I don't remember the first twenty years of my parents' married life as I was either too young or had not been born. Although I have heard hundreds of stories and incidents, I don't really know when or where they happened, so I will stick with things I remember (in most cases).

Watson and Betty (Nutter) Deitz first lived near Richwood. Then they built a house at Hominy Falls and ran a store there. Both places are in Nicholas County. Then they moved to Nutterville, just across the line in Greenbrier County, WV. This was where I was born and grew up. This home is still owned and kept up by my brother, Lawrence, although no one has lived there in thirty-five years, but we all can and do go there and move in extra a few minutes.

One story I remember hearing was about Mom taking the two oldest children by horseback to her parents' home about fifteen miles away. Just as she rode through a small settlement on Panther's Creek, a housewife opened a door and swept some newspapers out. The horse was scared and threw them off, injuring Mom. When someone rode back to tell Dad, he stopped them and described exactly what had happened and where. The messenger confirmed this. This sort of thing seemed to happen in the old days when people lived closer to nature, or was it ESP?

The older brothers used to laugh at Dad's habit of believing certain persons and taking their advice. They believed him to be very intelligent and more knowledgeable than they were, yet if there was someone who could talk in a very authoritative voice, Dad might believe the person, even though it might sound ridiculous to the brothers. They didn't believe some of these advisors to be half as intelligent as Dad, but they would sound as though they had most of the world's wisdom at their fingertips.

Since there was an age gap of seven or eight years between my next oldest and youngest brothers each way, I was Dad's main helper until his death when I was fourteen. Following is an account of what I remember about life on a farm and Dad.

Dad had no pain tolerance. It was a major event when he mashed a finger or got a bee sting. He would have a tantrum, but he had his own cures and medicines for everything and he applied them. We kept bees, and they would go out of their way a hundred yards to sting him. This was funny to me, as I could be surrounded by bees and never get stung.

All of us children were used to rough work and games

and thought nothing of it. He had grown up, maybe even rougher, but he never got used to it. We all had chores and long hours of work from the time we were very young. These things had to be done if we were all to eat. The girls were busy too: cleaning, washing, ironing, cooking, milking and a thousand other chores which have to be done around a farm. Much of the time though I was the only one at home to work outside with Dad and sometimes for my Grandfather Nutter, who lived at the next farm.

My father or grandfather never trained horses to pull a single plow to lay off rows for planting, or to pull a cultivator as they had the children to ride and guide the horse--mostly me! I remember the long hours of riding, riding, riding for either Dad or Grandfather. Dad had a habit, near quitting time for lunch or in the evening of suggesting that we quit, and then he would say, "Let's make one more round." Then there was another and another and another. I always thought the last twenty minutes lasted for hours.

Then there was the corn to be hoed. Sometimes Dad, a brother and a hired hand would be with me, but sometimes I would have the whole field to myself. This was the worst! I especially remember a large hillside field which I hoed all by myself. This field lay in sort of a curve so that I could see the whole field at once. I would make a round, which was about half a mile, and just be five feet up the long hill. I thought the whole world was planted in corn, and it was up to me to hoe all of it.

When I went to work in a manufacturing plant I thought that this work was play in comparison with farm work.

Actually, even corn hoeing was fun when there were other people to work with and talk to while working. Most of these people were hard working, entertaining, fun-people, who loved conversation and pranks, while hardly missing a lick of work.

My favorite job on the farm was looking after the sheep. It was my job on the way to and from school to go to a large, flat field on top of the hill and check on about forty to fifty sheep and account for all of them. I recognized all of them and gave them names of people I knew, imagining some facial similarity.

Some of these cold winter days the snow would be blowing sideways, driven by almost constant wind. I would be dressed to keep warm, and I loved a day like that. Maybe I was just different, or maybe it was the man against nature atmosphere, or maybe I was just looking forward to our always maintained big fire in the grate and a warm supper to go with it.

In spite of the hard work, our farm was a delightful place to grow up, especially during the shorter days in winter. People from other places stopped to stay over night: tax collectors, stock buyers and old friends. Dad might talk to his old friends most of the night there by the fire. Neighbors would come by to pick up their mail (there were no set hours for the post office to be open), and they would "set a while" to talk. Every night might be like a hunting lodge: everyone coming from a cold day, eating a large meal, and talking. Visitors always had stories of the old days and faraway places. I had never been more than a few miles from home. Dad would play checkers with me, and I almost never beat him, although I could beat a neighbor fairly often, who could beat Dad fairly often. Dad was real competitive. I never could understand how I could beat the man who could beat Dad, but I could never beat Dad. I remember Dad or the neighbor slapping their legs and laughing when they trapped the other one.

Dad was also a surveyor. The trouble was that although his work was almost professional, he would only charge a laborer's wages, even though he might have to travel several miles and plat this out afterward. I am still puzzled how he would figure out almost the exact acreage, which proved to be correct in later years. Later, I had a lot of higher mathematics, but I don't yet see how he did this without having been trained in geometry or trigonometry.

My brother, Granville, pulled a trick on Dad about his surveying one time. A lady called to ask Dad to survey a lot for her at Quinwood, where Granville was managing a store. Dad had her deed and calls, but he could not find a proved starting point or corner on her lot. He had to improvise by asking her neighbors for calls for their lots to find one with a definite proved corner marker. Finding this, he then had to survey past several lots, find the corner to this lot, and then survey it. Granville happened to come by and see this, and he realized the why or reason. He then wrote Dad a letter and signed the lady's first name, telling him that she had only contracted for him to survey one lot and not the whole town. This sent Dad into orbit, but before he could send a fiery reply, Granville had to confess, long distance, of course. Dad would be embarrassed to have someone think he would cheat anyone out of a dime, but that would be hard to explain to some people.

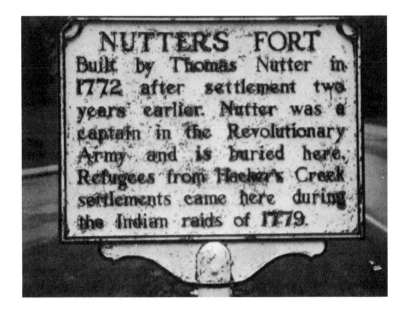

NUTTERS FORT
Built by Thomas Nutter in 1772 after settlement two years earlier. Nutter was a captain in the Revolutionary Army and is buried here. Refugees from Hacker's Creek settlements came here during the Indian raids of 1779.

To illustrate Dad's weakness for believing anyone who talked in a profound, authoritative voice, I will have to tell about my best school buddy, Frank, who was born with this type of voice. Frank was a slow learner, but he had the greatest imagination I have ever known. While he was still in the second or third grade, he couldn't spell a lick. The teacher would give him a word, and Frank would stand there, in his profound way, and say a number of letters, maybe not even one letter matching the word he was supposed to spell. With much help from the teacher he finally overcame this problem.

The older boys in the community would meet Frank and ask him about hunting or fishing, and he could instantly launch into a story as wild and exciting as any of the true stories of the mountain men of the early old West, like Jim Bridger or Kit Carson.

Frank, along with a younger brother and sister, would walk to our school about two miles. There were some cousins too. The girls at school would tease him unmercifully, just to hear his verbal responses. He might talk the whole gang into going to another school, which was about the same walking distance. There he would run into another type of problem. His girl cousin still talks about this. Although Frank was a verbal giant, he was a complete physical coward. They would start home with some neighbor boys that Frank didn't like, and he would start a verbal war. When the words lead to a fight, Frank would head for home, leaving her brother to fight all of them, even though Frank was bigger and stronger. Then Frank would talk the group into coming back to our school.

Once when Frank stayed all night with me, and we were sitting in front of a big fire, I got him started on one of those wild, comic, made-up stories. My Father was typing a letter when he overheard part of it. He stopped typing and asked to hear the rest of the story. Frank agreed and continued with the story, with it getting wilder and more comical, as he was inspired by having Dad listen. Dad sat there and laughed until tears ran down his cheeks, and he was slapping his leg. I sat there thinking to myself, "This can't be my smart Dad who has had Frank in school and has known him so long. Dad just can't be believing these wild stories." I didn't think anyone was expected to believe Frank's stories.

One of the drudge jobs I helped with on the farm was turning a grind stone for Dad and Granddad Nutter when they sharpened farm tools. During hay cutting season this turned into quite a job as the cycle bar on the mowing machine might have to be sharpened twice a day. It had a whole series of cutting edges, and I turned the grindstone for both of them.

I remember that I helped Dad on the farm, using methods which may never be used again. To plant grains like wheat, oats and buckwheat, the seeds were usually drilled into the ground, using a horse-drawn drill, which resembled a grass seeder used on lawns today. The big difference was that the farm drill had open metal feeders, which went a couple of inches below the top of the tilled soil.

In our country the feed drill was owned in partnership with several neighbor farmers, and they would take turns sowing the seed with it. Sometimes this led to problems. If the ground stayed wet until late spring, and the planting season nearly over, and our turn was low on the list that year, we went to the older method, which may have been used as long as people had been farming, for all I know. In broadcasting the seed, Dad would tie a small rope to the open corner and the bottom corner of the sack, leaving enough length between them to fit around his neck and shoulders. He would fill the sack with as much seed as he could carry and start throwing or broadcasting it by hand. I would set stakes in two rows across the end of the field seven steps apart in two parallel rows. He would sow up the inside of stakes, using them as markers, then back inside the other row of stakes. While he sowed that marked section, I would be moving the first row of stakes, seven steps past the second row, until the field was finished. A harrow was then used to get the seed deeper into the tilled soil. When the seed sprouted, I was always amazed to see how evenly he had sown it.

After the grain was cut and dried, a thresher came through and threshed it for a small share. The neighbors would exchange labor during threshing season.

Each farmer only planted an acre or so of buckwheat, so it didn't pay to have a threshing machine come back to thresh it. We used the method that must have gone back to the beginning of agriculture. The buckwheat was thrown on the floor of the barn, and a flail was used to separate the grain from the straw, and the straw was removed. The operation was repeated until of it was separated.

The flail was made with a pole about two inches in diameter and about five feet long. Another three or four foot pole, a little larger in diameter, was attached with a flexible leather strap, which you then flailed at the grain. Then we used what is now a very rare piece of machinery, which we called a windmill. It acted as a small threshing machine run by hand. The grain was poured into a box-like feeder with a heavy mesh screen, big enough for the grain to shake through it. When we started to turn the handle, the feeder would shake back and forth. A paddle wheel type of fan would blow the chaff out, and the clean grain would drop into containers.

Dad, with his wild, quick temper, could make some great threats when we irritated him, but when it came to actual punishment, he called for Mom. This wasn't often, as he had penetrating blue eyes, and when he looked at you over his glasses, under his bushy eyebrows, that was enough to wither the leaves on a tree.

It was great fun for us when he would have his glasses on his forehead and would start looking for them. He would give the whole family the devil for hiding his glasses, and, finally, one of us would lose our nerve and pretend to discover him wearing them.

Dad used to tell about a horse which he had on the farm one time which would balk and go backwards. Dad said if his head was on the other end, he would have had a really great horse.

This same horse is referred to in a story about Granville.

MY UNCLE EMERSON

My Uncle Emerson was my father's identical twin. He was one of the first citizens of Richwood, WV and was almost the first of everything. He was the first school teacher, the first JP, and maybe the first mayor and postmaster and half owner of the Deitz-Spencer store, which is still in operation.

Though they lived 25 miles apart, they remained very close until my father's death in 1928. I can still see my father, sitting in front of a big fire place, pounding out two

The Joseph Deitz Family, circa 1895

From a tintype circa 1895. Back row from left to right: Wade McClung, Uncle Emerson, father Watson Deitz, Betty Deitz, Vida Deitz, Etta Deitz. Front row from left to right: Jossie Deitz, Ernest Deitz, grandmother Virginia Ellis Deitz, grandfather Joseph Dickerson Deitz, Marvin and Mary, children of Matilda Deitz McClung deceased, and Fannie Deitz Beckner.

53

or three letters a week to Uncle Emerson, on an old Oliver typewriter.

When Uncle Emerson would visit, it was comical to see them talk. They would both lower their voices, each would hold up a hand beside his face and talk secretly about some business transaction. If you happened to overhear them, you would wonder what in the world was secret about the conversation. I can still remember seeing them, maybe a hundred yards from anyone or anything, talking with a hand beside their faces and apparently talking in low voices.

They were both athletic and very competitive, from checkers to any athletic event of the day. Old timers who grew up with them used to say that the Deitz twins couldn't be beat at anything athletic because they wouldn't be beat.

Uncle Emerson's sons were my age, and, until I was an adult and moved away to find work, I visited in his home. He liked to challenge me to play checkers and to tell jokes and stories. He was quite a jokester and tease, and he especially like to tease people who were quiet, good natured, and who enjoyed his teasing. He particularly liked to retell stories about this type of person turning the tables on him. One story was about a young fellow who had gone to work in the lumber mill and stayed in a boarding house. The young man would pick up mail for the people who ran the boarding house. Uncle Emerson was postmaster, and when the young fellow picked up their mail, Uncle Emerson, so to speak, got on his case. He would hand him their mail and make a remark about them letting just anyone have their mail.

One day when this fellow stopped to pick up their mail, Uncle Emerson gave him the mail and remarked (as usual) that he just couldn't understand them trusting their mail to such an unreliable person. That day he got a reply.

"They told me anything was better than leaving it with you," he said.

Another time when Uncle Emerson went rabbit hunting in Greenbrier County with a group of fellows, he teased one fellow all morning long until they all came to the house for lunch. When they went back outside and reloaded their guns, Uncle Emerson got someone to call the fellow aside and divert his attention while Uncle Emerson unloaded the man's gun. Then he began to tease him again and told him that even if the rabbits began to jump and run he wouldn't hit one, that he might as well stay at the house, etc.

Finally Uncle Emerson challenged him by saying, "I wouldn't be afraid to throw my hat in the air and let you shoot at it, for you couldn't hit it."

The fellow said, "Try it."

Uncle Emerson threw his hat in the air, and the man pulled both triggers on a double barreled shot gun, and Uncle Emerson's hat went into a thousand pieces. The man had reloaded his gun when Uncle Emerson's attention was diverted.

He used to tell of a fellow who was several bubbles off level and who used to come to church and testify, even though he had a mental handicap. One time he got up and, in his testimony, said Jesus has a heart as big as (groping for the right description) a slop jar.

Uncle Emerson's business partner was his brother-in-law, Shorty Spencer. Shorty told of the following incident as an actual happening.

Shorty and a department manger went to Huntington to buy dry goods during World War II. After their business was finished, they got in their car and were preparing to leave. The second car in front of them was trying to pull out, but it was pinned in by the cars in front and back. After maneuvering back and forward, the driver apparently lost his temper, shoved his car in low gear, and forced his way out, smashing the fender of the car in front.

The owner happened to be close enough to hear the crash and ran to investigate and saw his fender was smashed. Since there was such a shortage of car parts and mechanics at that time, the owner was really agitated and excited. He looked down the street, but the guilty driver was out of sight. When he saw Shorty and his friend in their car, he ran to them, real upset, and asked, "Did either one of you SOBs get that gentleman's license number?"

55

MY BROTHER GRANVILLE

Granville was the oldest in our family of nine children and was twelve years older than I, so he was away in school or working when I was growing up. I never really knew him when I was a youngster, but I was real close to him in my adult life as we lived close to each other for many years. We fished and hunted together a lot in my late teen years. My descriptions are my personal recollections, as well as many things other people told me. When I was young, I was always hearing about his ability to out-think, out-hunt and reach higher in athletic achievements, so I won't try to describe Granville from an outsider's viewpoint, but just from my own personal bias.

As I grew up I considered Granville the best at everything. As I grew older I broadened my view somewhat, but it didn't change much.

Before Granville went to Indiana to enter high school, he worked as a timber cutter to be able to pay board and room. He stayed with a cousin there. He made the football, basketball, and track teams as a freshman, although he had never seen a game played before. In fact, he had never even seen a basketball or football. He had worked in the woods at fifteen and sixteen years of age, and he was really tough. Nature gave him great quickness and lightning reflexes.

I used to grouse hunt with him along old log haul roads, and the grouse would take off with a roar of wings, darting around a tree as soon as they raised up. Granville's gun would go off before I could even move my gun. He never missed when I was with him. We always talked about why most shots were missed in this type of shooting. It is no wonder I thought he was the world's greatest shot. He was equally good with a rifle or a shotgun; however, most people are not good with both.

Bent Gum, Granville's brother-in-law, would talk about Granville by the hour and like to tell of the first time he met Granville, Granville went with his future wife to her home for Thanksgiving weekend, and her sister and brother-in-law were there. She had arranged for Granville to go rabbit hunting with Bent and some buddies at her home in Braxton County.

Bent had been a soldier in World War I and was a former state policeman. He quit and came back to live on a farm. Here came Maysel, his sister-in-law, bringing Granville along to hunt rabbits.

Granville was running a store at that time, and he appeared dressed in the latest hunting fashion: high top boots, some type of hunting pants, and a colorful checkered shirt. Bent was disgusted with this dressed up hunter, looking like an English lord, riding to the hounds, among the country boys. Bent said Granville had at least two strikes on him, as far as he was concerned. When he took a .22 rifle out to shoot rabbits, Bent considered that as strike three. Bent had to take him to meet his buddies with their shot guns, and he was disgusted and embarrassed. Then they started hunting, with everyone about thirty feet apart. Granville was next to Bent. No one expected Granville to kill a running rabbit with a rifle, but when a rabbit jumped up and went over the next rise and out of sight, Granville shot and said, "I think I got it." Bent decided then that this man was even worse than he had thought. To himself he said, "He shoots after a rabbit is out of sight and then says he got it." Not only was this strike four, but Bent was ready to shoot him. They walked around the hill, and there lay Granville's rabbit. Before the day was over, Granville had killed twice as many rabbits with his rifle as anyone else had with a shot gun. Bent became a believer. Bent would talk for hours about the shots he later saw Granville make on his farm, and he was always Granville's close buddy and booster as long as he lived.

Granville had hunted since he was very young, far out in unfamiliar woods, sometimes far from home, and he had worked in the woods, as well as helping to survey strange country. He had always taken nearcuts through strange country. I thought it was impossible to lose him. Then one day he and I had gone hunting, directly behind our home. We had gone down the hill behind the house, up the next long hill and were going to cross just over the top where there was a CCC fire trail so we could hunt along it. Before we got quite to the top, Granville spotted some grouse tracks in small patches of snow, so he bent his head toward the ground, watching for tracks. Instead of crossing the main ridge, the tracks led across a small ridge pointing back toward the creek, the way we had come. His head was down, and he didn't realize what had happened. I had my head up but just thought he was following the grouse tracks. Suddenly he raised his head and, real mad, said, "Where in the devil is that road?" I really got a kick out of that as I didn't believe he could be lost, even for a minute.

My father and Granville were more alike in temperament than anyone else in the family. Granville was the quickest tempered and more apt to say something funny when he was mad than when he wasn't, and he had a lot of good answers and quick comebacks just for fun. For instance, if someone mentioned that he wasn't very tall, he said he was real tall before he got married and settled down to his present height. He was more likely than Dad to take exception to insult, either imagined or real, and was ready to fight if necessary, as he had full confidence in his ability to take his own part.

When I first remember him he was more apt to use sarcasm or enticing words to get someone to say more than was meant to be said and then to hang him with his own words. Granville would then carefully point this out and get a great kick out of it.

He developed a trick shot with a .22 rifle. He would turn the rifle upside down, with the butt of the rifle on his forehead and shoot. He really got good at this. One time he happened by where some fellows were target shooting, and the shooter who was doing the best was letting the world know how good he was. Granville put on his act of not having shot much since he was a kid and didn't even know if he could shoot any more. At the same time he kept antagonizing the best shooter there, while sounding very innocent and about it not really looking like it was that hard a shot. Finally he had the man really challenging him to try a shot. Finally, seeming to be very reluctant and awkwardly handling the gun, Granville put it upside down on his forehead and shot, beating the man by a good margin. He probably did this many times.

My big brother was almost a living legend as a good shot with a rifle, pistol or shot gun. Stories about his shooting ability came from people who had seen him shoot and others who had only heard about him. Although Granville never said or believed that he was that good, he wouldn't spoil these great myths and legends. He loved to hear how his shots improved as they made the legend circuit, how much longer, and how much more difficult they were. I probably hunted with him as much or more than any one unless it was our brother, Lawrence. I have seen Granville make some unbelieveable shots, and I have seen him miss some fairly easy shots (for him). I saw him kill a running rabbit with a .22 rifle at 125 yards (I stepped it off to see). He just couldn't miss a grouse if I happened to be with him, but if I was out of sight, sometimes he would tell me about missing one and say I had to stay closer. I started going with him when I was about fifteen, and I know he could shoot and kill in half the time as the next quickest shooter I ever saw.

I remember seeing him use a single barrel shot gun and having an extra shell in his trigger hand. He practiced until he could shoot the second shot so quick you would swear that he was using a double barrel or a pump gun. I have seen him shoot one grouse maybe twenty feet in the air and shoot a second one before the first one hit the ground, and this while reloading for the second shot.

Once I was following him along a path through ice crusted snow when a grouse flew up, and he shot it while turning and stepping on icy footing. He turned, reloaded and shot a second grouse as his feet went out from under him. He killed the second grouse, although he ended up about thirty feet down the hill. I realize this sounds far fetched, but I saw it happen, and I was probably still trying to raise my gun when it was all over.

When my coaches would tell me I had quick reflexes, I used to think, "Great Goshen, you have never seen quick reflexes yet."

One time on the farm we were crossing a field to work. He had taken a pistol, and I had a shot gun. A grouse flew up, and we both shot, and it fell. Granville said, "Well, you got it." "No," I said. "I pulled past it." Sure enough he had hit it on the wing with a pistol. After all, how could he miss a grouse when I was along.

Granville always used to target practice on moving targets, mostly using still targets to sight his rifle in. He would shoot at destructive crows and birds on the wing. We would throw walnuts in the air to practice shooting. This gave us practice most people never tried, or, if they tried

59

it, they would give it up as impossible. Actually it wasn't as impossible as it sounds if you followed it carefully in flight. Most people gave up practice before they found the trick to it.

When some myth believer wanted to see Granville shoot, he had his upside down trick shot. When someone wanted to see the walnut or hickory nut shots, I would toss them up. He would tell me to throw the nuts in the air, making it sound as though I could throw them just any old direction or any old way. That wasn't how it was. While he was talking I would walk about twenty or thirty feet away and try to act as if I was tossing them in any old direction. Actually I would toss them underhand, directly straight up. This gave him an easy line to follow, and when the target got to the top of its flight, there would be an instant when it was almost a still target. That was when he would shoot and hardly ever miss. This was impressive to someone who didn't understand the trick. When the spectator got through telling it, you would think that the small target had jumped all over the skies.

Once in a while he would make a hundred to one shot, even for him, and he would get the most mileage out of this. One time I remember he stopped to see a man on business, and this hundred to one shot happened. The man was working with a group beside the road out in the country. About the time he got out of his car, a small ferry diddle[1] ran up a tall hickory tree to the very top and stopped, with the wind swaying the top limbs back and forth. Granville told the men he had a target pistol in his car, and he would take a shot at it. He knew it was an almost impossible shot, but why not try? To his amazement, when he shot, the ferry diddle dropped to the ground. He picked the animal up, saw that it was shot through the shoulders and started fussing about his pistol not shooting true. He told the men, "I don't know what is the matter with this pistol. I was shooting at its head."

I probably talked with Granville more than anyone else throughout our lives for as adults we lived closer to each other than any of the other family members. He was the only person I know who could tell the same story over and over and have it remain as interesting the last time as the first--almost.

When he moved to the northern part of the state on the Ohio River, some of my buddies and I would pick him up and go to Morgantown to see WVU play ball games. The first thing the boys would ask would be, "Are we picking Granville up?" They loved to hear him tell stories and would get impatient if someone interrupted, even if they were repeats, and they would ask him to retell stories.

The reason his stories were so interesting was that he was interested in everything and everyone. Sometimes I wouldn't see him for two weeks or a month, and he would tell things that had happened since we had seen each other. I would be all ears, but I realized that his experiences were routine except that he had seen new people and had heard new stories. If the story was interesting to the teller, it would be interesting to Granville. He could pass along a story and pass along his interest too without losing anything. My wife could listen to him for hours. Probably neither my wife nor I could have listened to the original story and heard anything of much interest, and I never could analyze this. I think that if I tried to retell one of his stories now and tell you they were interesting, you might say I was out of my mind.

One time when Granville was to meet someone at a certain time his car battery went dead. He got the car started and went to where he had bought the battery. He had a three year guarantee for a new battery, and he wanted the adjustment as the battery was only a year old. The battery department manager started giving him a hard time on the adjustment as he didn't believe the date on the guarantee was right, and he didn't have another one like it; therefore, he could not allow the full amount, etc. Granville was furious, for he was already late, and he hated to be late. He was always impatient over delays. After two or three hours the change was made and the adjustment was agreed on, with Granville paying the difference and getting his receipt. Then Granville remarked, with an air of innocence, that he really shouldn't kick as he had 40,000 miles on the battery. This was really a lot in those days. The manager blew his top, asking, "What in the h--- do you expect?" Granville answered him in a soft friendly tone, "Oh, that was all I expected, but you folks must have expected more as you were the one who guaranteed the battery for three years."

Granville was a truthful, honest person who just didn't want anything he hadn't earned. Because of this trait, the world lost a great con man. He felt it was a great challenge to run into a crook who tried to cheat him. He then had a chance to trade, no holds barred, and he loved to sell or trade with persons notorious for their grip on a dollar or a dime. This was for entertainment, as he would not waste his time on a person like that in a business way or to make a living.

He laughed at an incident that backfired on him. He was talking with a friend in a small town in Ohio, and he happened to look down and see a coin. He picked it up, and they examined it, agreeing they didn't remember seeing one like it before. Since neither of them was a coin collector, they didn't think this was very strange as they hardly ever took time to look at any coin. About this time they saw a notorious tightwad in town walking toward them, and Granville said to his friend, "You just watch me sell Mr. Harris this nickel for a dollar." His friend said, "That will be the day!" By the time Mr. Harris reached them Granville had his sales pitch ready and sold the rare nickel for a dollar.

A few months later the old Liberty magazine appeared, showing a picture of this nickel and told of its rarity and large value.

Granville was always active, fun loving and an achiever. When he was old enough to go to school, he could hardly wait to leave for school each morning. For the first two years he didn't miss a day of school, nor a day of Sunday School.

He liked to compete against others, and he thought of many ways to do this. Another race started by Granville was when Dad told the three older children to replant all the corn which had failed to grow. Granville suggested that each one see who could replant his row and get to the end of the row first. This worked very well a time or two, but as each one ran faster they were missing most of the empty corn hills. Later Dad thought the seed corn wasn't very good because so many didn't grow.

Granville often stayed with our grandparents who lived on the next farm. The roof on the backside of their house sloped sharply, and in the winter snow would slide off the roof and pile up at the back door in a big drift, and finally would almost fill the small back yard.

The chicken house was not far from the back of the house, and Grandma treated her chickens almost as well as she did the family. She never missed going out to feed them. One morning after a big snow, she asked Granddad and Granville to dig her a path through the heavy snow to the chicken house. Granddad had quite a sense of humor, so he and Granville dug a tunnel through the drifted snow to the chicken house. Then they sat back to get Grandma's reaction when she started out to feed her chickens.

The older children had the job of hunting the cows and bringing them in of an evening to be milked. At times this was quite a chore as the cows sometimes wandered through the nearby woods or over the hills, quite a distance away. The family had a horse named Old Rowdy, who was so stubborn that he had to be backed about twenty-five feet before he would go forward. However, he was a favorite with the children.

Granville suggested that they ride Old Rowdy to hunt the cows. This was fine on level ground, but, with two children riding behind, they began slipping off over the horse's tail when they went up hill. Granville solved this by turning Old Rowdy around and letting him go backwards, which pleased the horse, until the two who were slipping would slide back to their places. Granville guided the horse first forward, then backwards, until they reached the top of the hill.

This all took time, and Dad never did understand why they were so slow in bringing the cows home.

Granville was a good student and was ambitious to go to high school. Since money was scarce, he worked in the woods with a timber cutting crew in order to earn money to go to high school. Since high schools were scarce and far away, he decided to go to Indiana and stay with a cousin, which he did for the first year of high school. He had earned enough money to pay for his way by working with the lumber company.

Each day Granville left early for work and came back late in the evening since he had to go several miles. The family dog soon learned his routine, and each evening he would go about two miles of the way and wait to meet

Granville coming home.

Later Granville entered Nicholas County High School at Summersville and graduated there. He liked school and was especially interested in sports, particularly football. He also liked the debating team. On one occasion the school was having Parents' Day, and each class was competing to get the most parents out. Some parents lived so far away that a substitute could come in place of the parent. Granville wanted to do his part, so he asked his friend, Ruskin Wiseman, who had already graduated, if he would be his parent for the occasion. Ruskin could just see himself standing with the parents and hearing everyone laughing, so he turned down the request.

After graduation he and his uncle opened a store in Quinwood, which was a boom town at the time. He was here several years.

Granville loved to have family and friends come for a visit. He almost outdid himself as a host and liked to help his wife prepare the food or to take his guests to a favorite eating place.

At that time Mother was not teaching, so she did a lot of visiting among her children and friends. Granville decided on one occasion to write his Mother, but he didn't know where to find her, so he sent it in care of one relative and asked that it be forwarded. It was sent on and finally reached her, asking her to come for a visit. He said he was thinking of writing a story, "How To Keep Up With Mother."

Granville, in telling of something that had happened or that he had done, often added a humorous remark after telling it. Once, after being away from home for about a year, he returned home and one day saw some cows in the road near the house. He gathered some small pebbles and began driving the cows down the road. After going some distance he recognized one of the cows and suddenly realized that he was driving their own cows away from home. He drove them back where they belonged. When he told Dad about it, he ended by saying, "I apologized to the cows."

One evening Granville suggested to the other children that they have a contest to see who could get up, get washed, dressed, and be first at the breakfast table. All agreed. In order to be first, everyone began to sleep with their socks on, then underclothes. After waking up, they reversed the procedure and dressed first. Then some ran to a rain barrel back of the house, others to a wash basin or to the kitchen sink. With a quick dab or two to face and hands, they hurried to the breakfast table. The first one there was the winner. Mom noticed the children's unkempt looks and the rush to get to the table, which they had never done before. She soon caught on to the game, and that promptly ended the contest.

When Granville was in high school, debating was almost as much of a sport as football, baseball and basketball in competition with other high schools. With his love to compete, Granville was always on the debating teams, and his rebuttals were unmatched with his imagination. When an opponent made a point and gave his sources and authorities, he would reply by quoting an article from a noted expert, written three years before in maybe the Saturday Evening Post, giving the date of the issue.

The judges would be amazed at his recall of all of this quoting for the perfect rebuttal. This unbelievable memory came from Granville's imagination, with everything made up except the author. The judges or opponents never did suspect the truth.

He had a friendly feud going with his teachers. The teachers would often bring in pies and cakes along with some of the students who would have won some scholastic prizes and have a small party. Granville would manage to swipe a pie or cake, returning it later.

The teachers were determined to catch him because they suspected him. He was walking back to school one noon hour with one of the lady teachers who was wearing a rain coat on a day when one of the parties was scheduled. She told him that he wouldn't get anything that day as all of them would be watching him. He loved this challenge and went into the room where all of the teachers were ready for the party. They all began to tell him how he was being watched and dared him to try anything with them watching. While fussing with them about the unfair advantage they were taking of him, he slipped a cake plate underneath the coat of the teacher he had been walking with. This teacher, being a good sport, thought this was so funny she walked out of the room with the cake. When she finally left the room with the cake the other teachers were still telling him about their eagle eyes until they discovered the cake was missing, and he didn't have it.

THE DEITZ FAMILY

By Madeline Deitz

I have often heard people fuss that it seemed that they had married the (spouse's) whole doggone family. Well, I did, and I am glad. What an interesting, full of fun, experience this has been for the past forty-five years.

People have liked to tease me all my life: cousins, uncles and acquaintances, so I married into the right family. The teasing started the first day I met one of them. The brothers-in-law, the sisters-in-law's husbands, and the nephews today all tease. My wonderful mother-in-law liked to remind me of things I had done or said that she thought were funny. She never forgot the first time she visited us after we were married, and I fixed her a sandwich. When I served it, I remarked that the same sandwich would cost twenty-five cents over town. For the rest of her life, when I gave her a sandwich, she would always laugh and ask what the price would be in town.

My mother-in-law was one in a million, always good natured and fun. If I needed her, and we didn't have a car, she would find a ride or come by bus to help. I always told her that I never expected to be as good a mother-in-law as she was, but that I would always try. Our children always looked forward to her visits.

When my mother-in-law finally had to have someone stay with her, a lady named Amelia was found. Amelia told me, "Grandma won't hardly ask me to do anything." After nearly one hundred years of helping everyone else, she just hated the thought of needing help herself. When she was ninety-seven she was reading over one hundred books a year, and she could tell you anything in them.

Granville, my brother-in-law, was living out of West Virginia when we were married and did not move back for a couple of years. He immediately took up the teasing, using his entertaining imagination. One time his family and ours went to the family farm for a weekend. Even though I had been to the farm several times, he started telling me about the great Deitz "plantation" in the hills. I asked him if it had a bathroom, and he said, 'Oh, no, never would such a discriminating family use a beautiful 'plantation' home for such a dirty purpose."

Granville was a great host and would always be offering something special to eat or drink when we visited. Our children loved to visit them and get this special treatment, as well as the sightseeing trips and getting to listen to the funny things he would say or tell them. They still tell of the funny things he would say or describe when he would get mad or irritated.

Their favorite story was about what happened when we visited them after he was transferred to Kentucky. They had a small apartment with one extra bedroom, and the two girls stayed with them at the apartment. Dennis, our son, and I got a motel room some distance away. Granville was taking all of us to the motel, the girls going along for the ride. When we were all in the car except Dennis, who had gone back to check to see if our car was locked, Granville took off, talking to Dennis, who wasn't even in the car. After a couple of blocks, one of the girls decided we had better tell him that "Daddy is back at the car." The brakes slammed, and Granville said, "The devil he is!" He whirled the car around in a u-turn and went back to get him.

Granville had a light stroke the last year of his life and wasn't allowed to drive, but he really visited us more that year than at any other year of his life. He would stay for a week or so and go to see his doctor here. He would call us to say someone would bring him to Ripley, half way, and we would meet him there and then take him back. What an interesting week we would have!

My mother stayed with us and loved to watch TV in her room, but when Granville was here, she would quit watching TV and come in to listen to Granville talk all day. She would say, "Granville is good company." From her, that was equal to a ten minute speech from anyone else.

Granville would say, "Madeline, why don't you sit down with a cup of coffee and talk," He could just sit and talk about even the most common place things, and we would be spellbound. I would drive him to the doctor's office and wait for him. Most of these calls were routine, maybe to have his blood pressure taken or to pick up another prescription. With his impatience, he would come back irritated and mad with the red tape, and he would give me a word by word replay.

He was even funnier when he was angry. It would sound equal to going through the entire federal government to get a bill through Congress. There I was, giving him sympathy and cracking-up at the same time inside. This I missed when he passed away. The saddest part of his last year was seeing him slowed-up instead of on the run, doing everything quickly and efficiently. He was sometimes described as, "You know, the man with the short, quick step."

I have always told everyone that I felt sorry for anyone not married to a Deitz. My sister-in-law's husband, Ken, always told me and everyone else the same thing. When Ken died, the family lost their greatest booster, along with me.

Sometimes we would just decide to go to the farm. Almost every time most of the family would also appear with the same sudden notion. I called this the Deitz ESP. In forty-five years I don't remember any of them saying a cross word to me.

A few years ago when a family friend died, the funeral director came up and said, "This family acts like they hadn't seen each other for months." I told him that even if they saw each other every day you would think the same thing.

At one of those unscheduled farm gatherings, I was telling them about writing a newly-acquired niece and advising her to just jump into the family gatherings and talk as fast and hard as she could. Brother Lawrence turned to me and teased, "Madeline, you didn't do bad, did you?" I said, "No, I am just a fast learner.."

OLDEST MAN AND WOMAN IN GREENBRIER HONORED
BY TICE FLESHMAN
Date: June 28, 1976
Name of Newspaper: Beckley Post Herald

Rupert, WV. Approximately 130 persons signed the register for the Greenbrier County Senior Citizens bicentennial celebration held in the Rupert Community Center....gifts were presented to the oldest man and woman in the county. Prizes were given to Mrs. Betty Deitz, 95, of Quinwood, George Henderson, 81 of Rupert and Noah W. Williams, 95, of Charmco. Old relics were on display by different residents in the county.

The day began with the making of ice cream and an old fashioned butter churning, with everyone getting to sample the buttermilk. The butter and ice cream were kept for lunch to be served...butter for the homemade sweetened corn pone, corn bread, rolls and biscuits....

Alvin Meadows, who was a principal for many years in Greenbrier County, brought along several kinds of wood: green and dry to use in making toys the old fashioned way. He demonstrated his skill of whittling by making whistles, squirt guns, bows and arrows and spinning tops from wooden spools.

Mrs. Deitz, who was born Dec. 30, 1879, in Nutterville, started teaching school in Greenbrier and Nicholas Counties in 1898. She was married to the late J. Watson Deitz Feb. 23, 1901, in the Sugar Grove Methodist Church. They have nine children, 15 grandchildren and 16 great-grandchildren.

(Mrs. Deitz died in 1980 at 100 years and 6 months.)

BIRTHDAY A LETTER FROM MOM

Dear Dennis,

Your approaching birthday took my mind wandering back across the 60-odd years since the happy event.

Bad luck seems to run in waves and that must have been one of them. I hadn't tried my examination for teaching again, until 1912, when I was brought to that conclusion by so many things needing touching up and repairing at the old farm house.

With my first check I bought some lattice slats, had the cold underfloor underpinned and the lattice painted white. It was so pretty I stopped at the end of the lane every evening on my way in from school just to admire it.

My next check was pretty well spent to have shelves built in under the stairs where I packed my 500 and more jars of hard-earned fruit and vegetables.

Next step was to get the whole house painted white, and we bought the paint, but cold weather caught us, and we stored it in the attic where it fed the flames when the fire burned us out.

The fire in the parlor stove ate its way through the roof, and we only saved a few odds and ends but no clothing or bedclothes.

So here we were, in the middle of winter, naked. I must have been in shock, for I never begun to shed tears for three days. There we were, all seven of us, in on mom and dad.

In three weeks, with the help of neighbors, the hen house was built over, one big room 16 x 24, and we moved in.

Soon after, fate decided to add you to our fold.

That year was tough for all of us, you included. That walk through two miles of snow was no picnic to either of us.

When school closed in April, we decided the hen house wouldn't do any longer, so we planned the big house.

Watson was busy hunting lumber, farming and selling fertilizer. No one was old enough to be of much help, so you and I were kept very busy. "We" had to plant an extra garden and raise many extra chickens, for back then you

71

couldn't buy meat except slabs of fat bacon. With three steady carpenters, work hands, and company, there was no time left for play, you bet!

About the time this extra work started, the swarms of flies started coming into the henhouse, and the flat roof got hot, but the work went on, and soon the wild strawberries; how we all went after them!

We didn't have apples, but mom and dad had plenty; it kept Granville and Faye busy carrying apples that year. Then cherries come in, then blackberries, at last elderberries.

The pies that you and I baked in that fly-infested henhouse that summer would fill a boxcar.

As if the flies and the heat under that tin roof were not enough, all at once the real pest started–fleas by the millions! They gnawed and bit day and night. I sprinkled the beds plentifully with Black Flag...but that didn't help.

Then someone came along and said that salt would kill them. That did the trick, but we endured the pests for most of the summer.

Another problem was where to put the men to sleep. The old granary stood nearby, with a cellar which had fallen in, very damp or dripping wet. We moved two beds in that, and had to sleep on our dry clothes or they'd be too wet to get into in the morning. Then the drizzles started in, rain and more rain. At first the carpenters slept out there, but we had a whiz of a head carpenter and soon he had the frame of the house up, the roof on, and we moved out of the henhouse into the granary to sleep...

One day while we were picking blackberries among the loose rocks below the old sulphur spring, our bucket was nearly full when a loose rock turned, and suddenly we went sprawling on our backs among briers with inch-long spikes. I was covered with blackberries, and what a shrieking and scrambling to get back on our feet again!

On the Monday two weeks before your appearance, eight men were coming from Richwood to plaster the new house, three carpenters were still working at odds and ends, and there were seven of us. Watson came from church on Sunday and said, "Betty, I asked Felix and his family for dinner tomorrow." I nearly fainted. There were five of them, but when they came, Aunt Mattie and two little girls were along.

How could I cook in that henhouse for nearly 30 people!
On looking back to the summer of 1913, I wonder how you lived through it all. We hoped to get into the new house before you came, but luck again was against us. The plaster had to dry for two weeks before we moved in.

You cried for a month, and then you straightened out and grew into the nice and good man that you are.

But we hadn't much more than gotten settled into the new house when Granville and Faye let out the first big whoops; they had been exposed to whooping cough at school.

What a barking and coughing there was all that winter, but by and by things settled to normal, and life went on.

For Dennis, from Mother

MY MOTHER, BETTY NUTTER DEITZ

Mom was a school teacher, farm wife and mother of nine children. She was also the family doctor, and her cures and ingenuity took care of our ailments. The only time I remember a doctor being in the house was when a doctor was called for my younger sister who died of spinal meningitis. One time during my childhood Mom went to a hospital for an appendicitis operation. I remember her staying up all night applying hot towels to my ear for an earache. I just couldn't imagine all of us surviving without her as doctor and to comfort us.

She was the best teacher I ever had, and I had some real good ones. As a teacher she had her own inventive ways and methods of teaching. She was a great natural story teller and would teach history as an interesting story, and the whole eight grades in the one room school would sit and listen to every word, including the first graders sometimes.

One person told me about her being his teacher when he was only four years old. He would sleep in her lap most of the day while she taught and kept order at the same time.

In geography she would give assignments that challenged us to do a composition on an imaginary trip to places she assigned to us. We were to tell of the various places we would have to stop in order to get there, so we would have to study our maps thoroughly in order to do the assignment.

In spelling she would give us a list of words and tell us to do a composition using these words correctly. All her life she would tell of a trick I pulled on her with this assignment. I merely wrote that we had a spelling bee, and the following words were given to us to spell in the spelling bee. Then I listed the assigned words.

Since this fit her sense of humor and ingenuity, I was home free.

Mom's weakest subject was arithmetic, and it was my strongest subject. Dad was my sixth grade teacher, and arithmetic was his strongest subject. Then I had her for the seventh grade. Even when she was in her nineties she reminded me that she had found that if I came to her with a problem I couldn't solve she knew she wouldn't be able to solve it either, so she would say she was sure I could get it, and I usually did.

She enjoyed telling of her sneaky ways.

She was always a good manager on the farm, and even before Dad died he wanted her to do the bossing, unless we were actually working with him. She was firm, but she would challenge us to compete against ourselves. If, for instance, we would hoe a certain number of rows of corn, she would talk us into trying to hoe more the next day. We were always as proud to beat yesterday's record as we were of winning a ball game. If this failed to work, she would always find something equally effective, like a day off from work. Of course the day off would just happen to fall on a day when we couldn't work outside because of rain or something else.

Her ingenuity remained with her as long as she lived, but, unfortunately, so did her impatience to get work done. Safety precautions were dead last with her, and this led to some broken bones when she was past ninety. One time, after she had had a broken hip, my brothers contracted for someone to paint for her. She decided that she could rig up a safety belt with a rope, use a walker and paint as high as she could reach. Much to her disgust, she was vetoed on this.

When Mom was about ninety-five she decided to change some curtains and climbed on a chair. She fell while getting back down and broke an arm. One of my brothers made up his own version of how this happened. He said that she used a rocking chair arm, and when it didn't put her up quite high enough she placed a stack of books on the arm, stood on top of the books, and then fell.

She was disgusted that she couldn't write letters for a while when she had the broken arm.

Even though my brothers paid all of her expenses, she took great pride in saving on utilities and other things. She would always tell me that she saved some money every month from her small income. She would put her chair close to an oil furnace and turned it real low. The government would never have had an energy shortage if she had been in charge! My sisters would come into the cold house and fuss. My brother would tell them not to knock it when a ninety year old person never had a cold or was sick.

When she was ninety-seven she had surgery for diverticulitis and had to have a colostomy. She was not given a chance to live, but she lived three more years. She didn't like nursing homes and old people, even though those old people were twenty years younger than she. She couldn't stand their talk of trivial things and about the geniuses they had raised. She was still reading over one hundred books a year and was completely up to date on world events and affairs. When she was able she went back to her home, next door to my sister, Faye, who would cook for her and stay with her at night. My brothers would hire someone to stay with her in the day time, but when the person quit, she would decide to find help by telephone. No one could tell her the price being paid for this help, and in her call she would say how much she was sure the boys would pay. This would be about one-twentieth the amount being paid. This was embarrassing to some of the family and funny to others who didn't live close by them.

Mom was really upset when her eyesight began to keep her from reading as she hated TV and even radio.

As she neared one hundred, her hearing began to leave her. Some of us had the right voice pitch so she could understand, but there were other members of the family she couldn't understand at all. She couldn't understand me, even if I shouted, but she could understand my wife talking in a much lower voice, so she would talk by the hour to Madeline.

I would mostly listen to her as she liked to tell me stories of my childhood. She told of the time when I was old enough to get into trouble, but too young to tell her about it, although my wife doesn't believe that I was ever too young to talk. It seems that I had gotten into the silverware, and every piece of it disappeared. With her usual self-assurance she had all fifteen or twenty people who would usually appear for meals to eat with their fingers. After a day or two she found the silverware in a hole in the cabinet where I had dropped the pieces.

One winter Mom was to teach at a school about two miles from home, and, because she had had a serious appendicitis operation the summer before and couldn't ride horseback, she rented a small house near the school and took a younger sister and me with her to stay there from Monday through Friday that school year. The school house was about half a mile down a little used road from the house. One winter day a heavy snow fell, and she sent me to lead the way, along with some of the older pupils to break a path through the snow to the main road. That was her mistake! I led the way, zigzagging back and forth all the way to the main road, and when Mom followed with the younger children, the half mile had turned into a mile and a half. Since she felt I had showed imagination, all was forgiven.

She sent me to my Grandfather's on an errand when I was about five years old, and I went in a foul mood as I didn't want to go, for some children had stopped by our house. On they way I met a woman, a friend of Mom's, but I didn't know her as she lived six or seven miles away. As I was making my way along the bank by a rail fence in order to avoid a muddy place in the road, she stopped the horse she was riding and started asking questions just to tease me. Even though she knew me, she asked who I was and how old I was. I told her that I didn't know her and that it was none of her business who I was, and I didn't want to answer silly questions.

She stopped at our house to tell Mom about it because she thought it was so funny, and for years afterward she would remind me of the time I told her off.

Mom's inventive and unorthodox teaching methods never made the textbooks, and it would be difficult to write down what she might do on the spur of the moment, or as the occasion arose. She seemed to invent something that would hold each child's interest, but that might not work with any other child in the room.

One time a mischievous young boy caught some young mice and brought them to school. He had visions of seeing all the stories come true about the teacher jumping on her desk, and the girls would get up in their seats and scream. When Mom saw what he had, she invited him to come up front to show everyone such an interesting sight. She immediately made up an interesting story about a mouse escapade and a nature story about mice. The boy was enthralled with the story. I can't imagine her jumping on the desk because of a mouse, and maybe not a bear, for that matter.

During her early teaching experiences in a country school, at noon when the children were out playing, she saw two men approaching on horseback. They were the county school superintendent and his assistant. She was young, and she felt it was important to make a good impression in order to be recommended for next year. She rang the school bell early so these men could observe her teaching methods. Not one child responded, and she could not find them anywhere. Finally the men left. Was she embarrassed! About two hours later the children came straggling in and explained that they had seen the men and recognized them as school officials, so they disappeared through the brush and hid under a rock cliff. They thought the men were coming to give vaccinations, about which they had heard horror stories, and they weren't about to take a chance.

She always presumed that these officials never turned in a report about the school with the disappearing students and the young girl teaching to an empty school room.

In correcting children, both at school and at home, she was original and unorthodox. Mom had a theory that anyone could get too much of a good thing and acted accordingly. Once she was teaching close to our home and had a group of good students who liked to study and learn. She also had a little boy, Billy, who thought school was his enemy and was willing to retreat from it. One nice sunny day, when he caught Mom's back turned, he climbed out an open window and went home. His mother believed in learning, much to his disbelief, and sent him back the next morning with his sister. Mom made him climb back out the window, come around to the front door, then climb back through the open window again and again, until he thought an open window was more of an enemy than a school room. She then originated a learning process to keep Billy's interest.

One of my teachers started teaching fractions, and he drew an imaginary pie, cutting it up in six pieces and showing how two-sixths equalled one third. That was clear and understandable, and it gave me an idea for a trick on Mom. That evening I told her about this and said the drawing wasn't as clear as using a real pie and actually seeing it cut up. She used a real pie, cutting it up, and explaining as she went along how two-sixths equalled one third. I told her that now I understood, and I was sure I would if I ate the third used in the demonstration. Of course I didn't really have to go around Robin's barn to get pie as we were free to eat anything in the kitchen that was available. It just made the pie taste better to use this method, and she liked this type of trick even better than I did.

When she neared her one hundredth birthday I asked her if she could remember the names of pupils in her first school as a teacher. That was before 1900 in a school of more than forty pupils. She said, "Of course, and I can tell you where all forty sat." I have no doubt that she could.

It is said that older people remember things of long ago better than things that have happened recently, but that was not true with Mom. She could tell you all about each one of the hundred books she read each year, and I know she was right, for I read many of the same books. I took her many books as I knew just which books she would like.

Mom was equally good at handling children and grandchildren. One day she was sitting for two grandchildren who were about four or five years old. They hadn't had her as boss too much at that time, and they decided she wasn't their boss and were determined to do battle over authority. What a mismatch! She had fixed dinner and called them to eat. They climbed a small tree and refused to come down. She told them that if they wouldn't come down she would have to burn the tree, so she got some newspapers and pretended to be about to start a fire. They beat her to the dinner table.

There was one way Mom changed during her lifetime. When we were growing up she had all the confidence in the world that we were capable of doing anything, from taking care of the mail, re-routing it, or looking after the telephone central at a very young age. She gave very little advice as we grew up--not many do's or don'ts. I think that if one of us had come to her and told her we had money to visit New York or Chicago, she would have encouraged us to do so, as it would be a great learning experience. She would have very little doubt that we would make it fine, even if we were only ten years old. By the time she was ninety she smothered us with advice, and she worried about any possible problems we might have, or that she could imagine we might have. If a problem was mentioned to her, when you saw her again, she would have an answer, even though you might have forgotten about the problem.

We had fun teasing her about this. My brother Harold used to stop by and apologize because he hand't had time to make out a list of things for her to worry about, but he would get around to this soon.

Mom had a close friend who corresponded with her over the years, and one day she received a letter from her friend, which said, "Well, Betty, you will soon be one hundred years old. Then, no doubt, Jesus will soon be coming for you."

Mom was determined to live until her hundredth birthday. The family was planning a big celebration, with friends and relatives galore, and there was a big, beautiful birthday cake, with ten candles, one for each ten years. Mom was having a ball! She had made the grade--one hundred years! She had done herself proud.

After all was over came the relapse. There was no goal left. She gave up. She couldn't do anything for herself. Night and day she called someone to hand her a drink of water from the glass by her bed because her arm (which had been broken years before) was too short to reach the glass. Someone had to turn her over in bed because she wasn't able to turn herself. She was helpless.

After a week she realized that she was going to live, so she began to reach for the glass of water and to turn herself in bed. She could do the things for herself that she had always done. She was back to normal.

After a life time of being ready on time and being impatient to leave, apparently she decided Jesus was not ready to come for her, as her friend had written.

Mom died at one hundred years and six months and was buried at the End of the Trail Cemetery at Clintonville. She had had nine children, 25 grandchildren, 3 great grandchildren, and one great great grandchild.

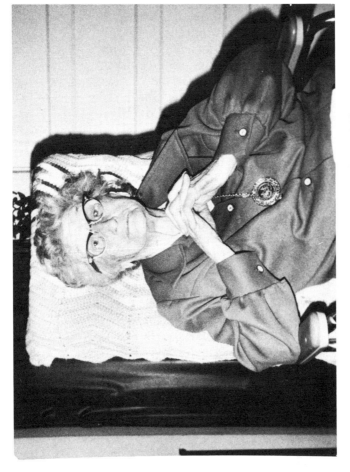

Betty Deitz on 100th Brithday, 1979

MY OLD ROCKING CHAIR AND I
BY BETTY DEITZ

We two just suit each other
In one way or another
We have lived here long together
Through fair and foul weather.
We feel old enough to die
My old rocking chair and I.
We have grown long out-dated
And very much dilapidated.
When we rock our joints creak
When we talk our voices squeak
We are here quite, quite alone
Where it is quiet as a stone.
When we cannot sleep at night
Our little fire burns Oh! so bright.
We can move up where it's warm
Don't have to use a special form.
Then we can do a little thinking
And a little coffee drinking.
We can look back o'er the years
With their joys and with their tears.
Sometimes we gaze into space
When the sky is all like lace.
We watch the stars in sky a-twinkling
And Old Man in the Moon a-blinking.
When we think about us two
Neither of us real brand new.
My chair is covered with a spread
Taken from off my only bed,
With pillows stuffed into its side
Just because it's grown too wide.
But it suits me to a tee
For there are things wrong with me,
Something really within my head
You have noticed as you read.
I think my hair may be all messed

And I never looked good at best.
But we are glad that we can think
   Though our eyes do blink and blink.
We know we are old enough to die
   My old rocking chair and I.
Will we then just melt away
   Like the 'old one-hoss shay'?
Soon we'll hear our Master calling
   Into deep sleep we'll be falling.
When they take me over there
   Will they take my old, old chair?
Or they'll say it's excess freight
   And it will just have to wait.
If it should be later sent
   I would want it in my tent.
Or if under a tree I sit
   It would mean to me a bit
To be together, my chair and me
   And this you can plainly see.
This could happen any time
   Neither of us worth a dime.
We are old enough to die
   My old rocking chair and I
But the Hand that stilled the sea
   Will sustain my chair and me.

MY GRANDMA

By Larry Deitz

My Grandma, Betty Deitz's life span covered a century. It started in the days of horse and buggy and riding sidesaddle, and ranged up through the invention and development of automobiles and airplanes; it spanned the Spanish American War, two World Wars, the Korean War and the Vietnam War; it covered the space program era with the moon landing and space walk; it ran through the Great Depression and on up through Watergate.

But the period of time that I knew her covered approximately three decades in which our life spans overlapped. It is upon this period that I thought it might be good to write my memories of Grandma from a grandson's perspective.

We called her Grandma or Grandma Betty; she didn't like to be called Granny and Grandmother didn't fit.

When Grandma was in her seventies and eighties, she made it a practice to visit for periods of time with her sons and daughters, living a few weeks or months with various ones of them, but not staying too long with any one of them. I remember that her coming was not announced too long beforehand, at least not to me, it was usually just heralded by a comment that Grandma was coming for a few days and shortly thereafter she would arrive or Dad would go and bring her. She would spend a few weeks and then her departing would be about as quick. She would ask Dad when he could take her to her next chosen destination and he would pick a date. The morning of her departure she would emerge from her room with her suitcase packed, hat and coat laid out, and would announce that she was ready and would not be one to keep Dad waiting. This was her way of subtly applying pressure to get on with the trip. This tactic probably worked on most of the family, except Dad. The reason it didn't work with him was that it didn't have to, since he was like her; that is, always in a hurry anyway to get wherever he was going or on with whatever he was doing. I remember that no amount of persuading on my part would convince her to stay any longer than what she had in mind.

It was always an exciting event for me to learn of Grandma's impending visits. Her visits meant many things, a few of which were noon lunches at home from school, lemon pies and stories.

My mother was a school teacher and was away from home during the day, so I had to carry a lunch box or eat the hot lunches of the school, except when one of Grandma's visits rolled around; then I would be allowed to come home and eat at noon. Grandma's lunches were a work of precision. She always had it timed to the minute when I would hit the door and the food would be laid out steaming hot on one plate with utensils and the rest of the kitchen cleaned up with no evidence that any cooking had gone on. The amount of food was generally the amount that I would eat and might typically consist of a grilled cheese sandwich, a bowl of soup, large glass of milk and, from time to time, a large slice of lemon pie. Occasionally, she would serve a little too much of something - that is, something other than lemon pie - (I don't think you could serve too much of that) but when this would happen she had a remedy, she would simply say "eat it to get shut of it" and I, like all growing boys, was never full, so I would take care of it.

The only foul-up in her lunches that I can remember came one day when she accidently poured buttermilk over my bowl of rice. I always loved sweetened cooked rice with milk and I was so caught off guard that I gagged. I know it was an accident, since she got another bowl of rice from the refrigerator and put some sweet milk on it, but knowing Grandma, she would have been likely to have improvised by using buttermilk with a lot of sugar had sweet milk not been available.

The lemon pies were a connoisseur's dream. Her cooking method was very simple, she just opened the box of commercial pudding and pie filling and mixed up the ingredients. She never followed the instructions on any box. I am sure of this because she never followed instructions from anybody for that matter. The meringue on the pie would stand soft and fluffy with toasted brown areas and beads of golden syrup discernable here and there on top. Her meringue was so different from the shriveled up, tasteless pie I encounter in restaurants today. The fact the meringue was so fluffy and soft was not so much her special cooking techniques, but in the fact that I consumed them before they had a chance to deteriorate. In writing all of this, I must confess that the reason her pies tasted so good is more due to my nostalgic memory than due to her cooking abilities.

Story telling was another thing that characterized Grandma's coming. She had a whole variety of stories which were always interesting. They were composed of past happenings in her life, history, nature and fabrication. Sometimes a little of each showed up in her stories. Many of the stories were from past events, but probably were embellished a little for story telling purposes. Her renderings might involve wading snow-drifts, a brother charged by a cow with horns, or her being thrown off of a horse. They involved things like mad dogs, bears and catamounts. Now, I'm not exactly sure what a catamount was. I suppose it was nothing more than a West Virginia bobcat, but it existed back in Grandma's childhood days and would cry in the darkness and would be heard making footsteps in the leaves of the lonely nightwoods. Being the small kid that I was I envisioned a catamount as being about twice the size of a tiger and being much more ferocious.

Blending my childhood memories and Grandma's stories leaves me with the impression that our family never owned a horse that hadn't thrown Grandma. She was always carrying one of her babies (my aunts or uncles) which was miraculously thrown unharmed into a nearby snowbank or bush with Grandma sustaining only minor injuries such as a broken leg or arm.

Her bear stories were my favorites with the fire bear being the capstone of them all. This was one that my mother objected to being told after dark, since it might cause me to have bad dreams, but nonetheless, it was my favorite. Try as I may, I cannot recall the details of the story, but the jist of it was that there was a wild maruading bear with eyes of orange fire that could be seen in the dark and that had smoke coming out of its mouth and it terrorized the community by killing livestock and endangering the inhabitants. Finally, the men of the town tracked the bear, entraping it in a cave, and when one of them attempted to shoot it, the result was a terrible explosion. To my knowledge that exposion resulted in the extinction of all fire bears, as I have not seen them listed in any zoological or national history publications.

Grandma's sleeping habits were a hallmark of this period of her life. She went to bed early, even before dark, say 7:30 p.m., and would rise about 6:30 a.m. She would also take an afternoon nap which probably contributed to her good health and longevity.

It was during one of these afternoon naps that I eluded her watchful eye, much to my consternation. I was probably preschool age and had been riding the range of the backyard with my next door neighbor and sidekick, Mikey. Being the good cowboys that we were, we decided we needed a campfire and I was elected to secure the matches. I stole into the house and pulled a chair to the sink top and climbed up and got them from a metal box that hung on the wall. Grandma aroused enough to call and ask what I was doing, but my answer of "nothing" apparently satisfied her and I returned to the western wilderness of the backyard. When the campfire was lit, it went like wild fire. I might also say it resulted in sparking some additional fire of its own from both our fathers, but regardless of that, the inferno raged up through the dead brush toward Mikey's house. A neighbor lady called the fire department which drew the battle line between the fire and the house and stayed off the additional impending disaster. Everything was finally secure; that is, everything except Mickey and me. In later years, Grandma would ask me if I recalled the event. Of course I recalled it, Dad had forcefully explained the shortcomings of repeating such an act.

While I was at school and Mom and Dad at work, Grandma was home occupying herself with light house-work, reading, taking afternoon naps, and preparing the meals. It was an unspoken rule that Grandma was not to go upstairs by herself. This was for her well-being be-cause of her age, and because no one wanted her to fall, nor did anyone want her to be alone if she did fall. So for her own safety, it was generally understood that she was not to go upstairs. However, Grandma was not one to be dictated to in any fashion and there was, from time to time, telltale evidence that she had made excursions to the upper level during our absences. This was never conclusive, not enough to cause confrontation, but enough to let people know somehow, someway, something was not exactly kosher. It could be in the form of a book moved from the upstairs to the downstairs or a piece of furniture displaced slightly, but, in any event, it was enough to cast cause doubt and suspicion; maybe just enough evidence left behind that she could take pride that she had prevailed under the circumstances. She did not believe she was too old to do such things, after all, she did not believe herself to be middle aged until sometime around her seventy-fifth to eightieth year.

Grandma invented child psychology long before Dr. Spock even noticed kids. She would recount to me how I took my new tricycle and ran over her toes thinking this was great fun when I was little more than a toddler. Not responding to her requests to stop she sat me down and ran over my toes with the tricycle. This did not harm my feet, but it apparently did alter my driving habits.

A young cousin of mine (her grandson) once threatened to run away from home. While he was packing his clothes, Grandma handed him a dollar and explained that he probably would not get beyond Charleston by nightfall so he was to be sure to get a taxi and ask to be taken to the Union Mission to spend the night. This caused the little fellow to break down in tears saying if Grandma did not care whether he left, nobody cared. His exit ended then and there without him even reaching the threshold.

Some of my most cherished memories of Grandma centers on the time she kept house for me while I worked a couple of summers at "The Farm", the name given to the old Deitz homeplace. A few times we talked of christening it with a more descriptive title like other people who use such names as the Ponderosa, Willow Estates, Oak Grove and the like, but always nothing seemed to fit like"the Farm" so "the Farm" it is. My Dad had planted some seventy to a hundred thousand pine trees to keep the place from growing up. A portion of these had to be pruned each summer as they were sold for Christmas trees to keep the taxes paid and maintenance performed on the place. During these summers, it was my job to prune these trees to get them shaped in some manner for future sales. Some of the neighbor boys would help during the day but none would stay overnight. They would work all day, but then go home. Grandma stayed with me during these summers and it was her job to do light housecleaning and cooking. It was my job to work in the fields. Grandma would have been around eighty years old and I was close to being a freshman in high school. This was a great experience for me having grown up in town and only prior to this having visited "The Farm" on weekends. This was the first time I had free range of the place, pretty much on my own. Dad expected eight hours of work each day, the rest of the time was mine. Of course, the summer days were long with the nights short, so I had ample time to explore and roam.

The first night that Grandma and I spent at the farm was unusual for me. She slept downstairs and I in one of the three bedrooms upstairs. I had never experienced sleeping in an old abandoned farm house before and it was quite an experience. Grandma went off to bed and went to sleep and that was that. For me it was something different. I laid awake that night listening to all the various sounds that were unfamiliar to me--- the chirping of the crickets, the various insects bumping into the window panes and the sound of bees buzzing around inside the room with me wondering if they would at any time drop down in among the bed clothing. It did not seem to matter how many of them I swatted, they were always quickly replenished. There were sounds of the creaking and cracking of the house, sounds of the refrigerator kicking on and off, and the sounds of mice scurrying around in the walls and attic. I locked the doors securely when I went to bed, but with all these unfamiliar sounds I had visions of being attacked by an intruding prowler or a thief or a ghost or any other thing that my imagination could cook up. However, this was only a one-night occurance, as being tired after working in the fields all day and becoming familiar with the sounds, I never worried about them any more except for the bugs flying around the room - I never did quite like that aspect of it. After that first night I did not always lock the doors. Grandma never locked the doors or even mentioned it. After all, she had grown up in a time when people did not lock doors and did not have to lock doors. Looking back now, considering how times are, one would consider it foolishness not to have locked the doors before retiring. But the truth is that the locks were probably not strong enough to keep anyone out and had they gotten in, they would never have been detected among all the other sounds that were going on.

Pruning pine trees is pretty hot business, standing looking up into the sun. I remember I got fried several times and always carried a red face during these periods. There are other hazards of pruning trees; they include getting the sticky gum all over you, getting pricked by the millions of needles encountered, meeting up with an occasional snake and the dread of all dreads - hornets. Some of the fields had not been planted in the most orderly fashion. Some of the trees had grown into each other and were somewhat dense in places and sometimes you had to push your way through just to get from one tree to another.

It was always my constant fear of pushing my way into an unseen hornets nest, which did happen periodically. Once the commotion died down, I would have to sneak back to the closest trees and gingerly prune them, lest the disturbance should reoccur. Grandma, having the medical expertise that she had, was responsible for taking care of all the minor medical emergencies such as bruises, cuts, sunburn and bee stings.

My way of doing business was to get up early and work until a predetermined breakfast time, then work until noon, take an hour off for lunch, then work until about three or three-thirty in the afternoon. Getting the eight hours done in the soaking dew of the morning was preferable to working in the blaze of the evening sun; besides it left the late afternoon and evening free to wander over the woods and meadows of the place.

After getting cleaned up and eating supper, I would take my .22 rifle and look for an unsuspecting ground hog or crow. I knew every ground hog hole in sight, when the chucks sunned themselves and when they fed. Dad prohibited the shooting of game animals in the off-season and prohibited the shooting of song birds, but any other critter with four legs or feathers was fair game. It seems now somewhat of a waste, but back then I religiously hunted the ground hogs and crows. The ground hogs were given to a neighbor who fed them to his dog and the crows were hung in the garden.

You couple this free time with the fact that Grandma went to bed early and you can see I had a good bit of time to myself.

Two of these nimrod adventures I remember in particular. One was the day I encountered a skunk grubbing his way along in the big meadow. I stalked in as close as feasible (from the up wind side), took careful aim, shot and quickly retreated, expecting the skunk to return the fire. The shot must have been well placed because it "killed the skunk so dead" it didn't stink. I circled the dead varmint a few times testing the wind and finally concluded it was safe to approach. With a handy flat board, holding it at arms length, I carried my trophy to the house to show Grandma. She did not appear to share my same enthusiasm, but did show enough interest in it so as not to disappoint me; however, in her parting remarks on the animal, she tactfully suggested that I deposit the thing as far away from the house as possible. I suppose she expected some delayed reaction.

The other incident occurred one day at noon as I was returning to the trees. I spotted a snake in the lawn and quickly retreated to get my trusted rifle. Approaching cautiously, I took careful aim and fired. Nothing happened. I changed positions and fired again. Nothing happened. Being the expert shot that I was in those days, especially at a range of ten feet, quite puzzled I moved in for a closer inspection only to find the snake was already dead, having been run over by automobile traffic going in and out of the yard as it was our practice to park near the house. Grandma, having watched the whole episode from the front porch, was quite amused and in later years would ask me if I recalled the time that I "killed the dead snake."

Prior to Grandma's declining years she spent much time reading and writing. She enjoyed the Bible as well as many books, biographies, autobiographies, and histories. When I say histories, I mean histories from our standpoint. Considering her longevity, reading history to her was probably just brushing up on some past current event that had transpired during her life, which she could recall being discussed at the time with family and friends. After all, her life span covered portions of the terms of twenty presidents.

She wrote many poems, stories, and letters. One aspect of a long life which must have caused her pain was to see those whom she had corresponded with, one by one, die off. This did not deter her letter writing, in as much as she turned more and more to her grandchildren and great grandchildren as her correspondents. One of my prized possessions is an unread letter which she wrote to my infant daughter. It arrived in an envelope addressed to me and within was another envelope marked "To Christy, do not open until seventh birthday". I suppose the Post Office, had they known one envelope contained another envelope, would have liked to have had another stamp purchased out of the deal, you know how technical bureaurats are, but nonetheless, they were outfoxed and the letter got through. This letter is wrapped in plastic and is locked in my safety deposit box at the bank. The scheduled opening of this unorthodox time capsule is 1985. I don't expect anything earthshaking or profound but it does reflect Grandma's way of extending herself beyond the grave and touching a generation that she knew she would not have an opportunity to get to know.

In Grandma's last few years of her life she was not told about the death of relatives and tragedies within the family for fear of worrying her in her feeble condition. I never agreed with this philosophy, after all, a person who lives to that age has to be pretty tough, but since I was only a periodic visitor, I did not believe it my place to object. However, this situation created some difficult situations, since the visitor would have to keep abreast of what she had not been told. On occasion she would inquire about a deceased and one would have to mumble something like "I haven't seen him for a long time" and hope that she would change the subject. Of course, she didn't always change the subject but would recount her last time of seeing the individual and inquire of a known ailment or of their general health. This was her way of exploring deeper without being direct. This would cause some tense moments and one would have to change the subject rather than tell an untruth or spill the secret. I was never convinced that she did not suspect something but she never forced the issues to their ultimate. Upon Grandma's entrance into heaven it is supposed that this practice caused some confusion as she inevitably met some folks up there that she supposedly had left behind. From what I understand, though, there will be ample time there to get all the facts straightened out.

Grandma always enjoyed electrical storms. When most

people had thoughts of getting into feather beds or staying away from water pipes or sitting in automobiles for safety, Grandma had thoughts of opening the drapes and pulling a chair up to the window to get the better view. She would have viewed them from a tree top if she could have figured a convenient way up.

It was a July day in 1980 as I stood in my office well over two hundred miles from her that I watched an approaching electrical storm and, knowing of her deteriorating condition, my thoughts turned from my work to her and her thoughts turned from this earth. I learned later that her death had occurred at approximately the same hours. It seemed quite fitting to have been reminded of her in such a way.

As we gathered to lay her to her final rest, there was the feeling that she would be missed by all. At her age we had come to expect losing her and to count each day that we had her as a blessing. She had resigned herself to departing, having reached her last final goal, that being to live to see her one hundredth birthday. Her failing eyesight and failing hearing in her last few years seemed to be the hardest of all for her to endure. It had all but cut her off from the things she had held dear--reading and communicating. She would frequently remark that it was "awful to grow old and get in such a fix". I stood at the funeral home, feeling the loss, but knowing that when a person lives to be a hundred years old you don't feel compelled to inquire of the Lord why he didn't see fit to extend her life just a little longer.

Today as I observe able-bodied men who refuse to work, men who strike because they think they can't live on salaries five to six times the minimum wage, when I see school buses dropping off children every two hundred feet so they don't have to exert themselves walking, when I see young people with every advantage, ungrateful for what they have, I can not help but contrast them to Grandma's life of hardships, of raising nine children, of providing in hard times, of walking miles to teach school in all weather, of her determination to keep herself intellectually active and mentally alert. I draw strength in having known her.

As I look around it appears to me that there are few people today of her character to stand up and fill the ranks.

AUNT ROSA

Aunt Rosa, my Mother's sister, who was two years older than Mother, played a big part in my growing up years. She had no children of her own, so she often borrowed a niece or nephew for a few weeks to a few months at a time. I was one of the ones often borrowed until I was of school age, and also old enough to be needed on the farm to carry and fetch.

She and her husband, Uncle Marvin O'Dell, lived at Hominy Falls in the first house my parents had built, a white cottage with four columns on the porch. What a pretty house that was there on the knoll! There was a white picket fence all they way around the yard, with flowers planted inside the fence. The country road was about fifty yards in front of the house, and there was a cement walk from the front gate to the porch, which was a perfect place to ride my little red car with pedals. Near the porch were two large oak trees with a porch swing between them.

About half a mile below the house, Hominy Creek made a half circle around a sloping open field, creating a view as though it was from a picture or painting.

There was a train track following along the creek, and I would hurry to the back porch to climb on the bannister to wave to the train crews, who always waved back. Aunt Rosa and one of the crew members always teased me about the time I hurried from the out-house to the bannister to wave at them when I was not properly dressed for company.

One time I went to stay with Aunt Rosa and Uncle Marvin for a while at Hominy Falls, where they had a general store for about twenty five years. They would buy me more toys than I had ever seen!

The most exciting trip of my life was when Aunt Rosa took me to Richwood by log train. While we were there, they bought me a manufactured, painted sled, and she said I made her pull me on the sled through the crowded Richwood streets all the way back to the house where we were staying.

We stopped after night at the little lumber town of

Curtin, WV. Since I had never seen any more lights at one time than two or three kerosene lamps, it was more impressive than seeing all of New York city at night later.

The first soft drink I ever saw was at Aunt Rosa's. She had purchased a few cases for the first time and offered me some to drink. I had heard Mother and Granddad Nutter discuss the evils of whiskey, and I thought she was trying to get me to drink whiskey, so I totally refused.

I always loved the early mornings and hearing the rooster crowing from the Rader farm across the creek.

I remember Uncle Marvin's Uncle Granville O'Dell whistling early in the morning when he was inspecting the farm, which was nearly a mile away. He could whistle a tune, and the whistling would sound as clear as though it was only a hundred yards away. In those days almost every man whistled as he worked or walked. Where did all the whistlers go? No one seems to whistle any more. The women did not whistle as they believed the old saying, "A whistling woman and a crowing hen never come to a good end."

The grist mill was just below their store and about a mile away from the house. I liked to watch the miller, Em Orndorff, run the water-powered mill, and I especially liked to watch the older boys ride the swift water on their backs down the mill race. They would grab the cross pieces nailed across the top when they neared the mill. If they didn't stop they would drop on the mill wheel and go on to Hominy Creek below the falls of Hominy Creek.

Aunt Rosa was active in the church, and one time when there was a ministers' convention at her church, she came home and told me that they were all coming home with her for dinner. I was petrified. I had heard many hell fire and brimstone sermons, and here I was one little sinner among all those preachers. I was sure I would be raw meat to a group of preachers, so I began to campaign to go to play with a neighbor's boy, and I just had to go that day. After some debate, Aunt Rosa asked, "What is the matter? Don't you like preachers?" My answer was, "I like preachers, but I just don't like to be crowded with them."

I was subject to migraine headaches all my life, and I had one while I was there, really suffering and feeling deathly sick. Aunt Rosa had some strange theories, and she explained to everyone that I was homesick. Didn't she know that I was just plain sick?

Uncle Marvin and Aunt Rosa were the greatest example I ever knew of the belief that opposites attract. Uncle Marvin was easy going, good natured and didn't like to make decisions. I never saw him mad or even irritated, and I don't remember him ever saying an unkind word to me. He once served a term as deputy sheriff in Nicholas County--that was a square peg in a round hole if there ever was one! If he ever made an arrest I never heard of it. Carry a gun? I don't think you could have gotten him to pick one up. We used to say that if he had met a man and had a warrant to arrest him for a robbery, he would have warned the man to leave before the sheriff saw him.

Aunt Rosa helped keep the store, could cook dinner for a dozen people on short notice, be a church and missionary society leader, a Red cross leader, minister to the sick, and make decisions in a minute. The decisions would be from highly intelligent to very unorthodox.

She charged into ministering to the sick with all guns flaming. She poured medicine into the patients, had them up, had them down, used hot towels, and used cold towels. Then she couldn't understand why they didn't arise from their death beds and go back to work after a few hours.

The only personal experience I remember from her nursing was when I stayed with them when I was going to high school. One day I stayed home from school as I had the flu or something. She was running a boarding house by this time and was really busy. I was in bed in a room where there was a pot belly stove. The fire got low, and she came in, saying the fire was going out. She stoked the fire and got it going full blast. Thirty minutes later she returned, asking why I had let the room get so hot. She then shut off the damper, raised the window, opened the stove door, and went out. In another thirty minutes she returned, wanting to know why the room was so cold. So, again she added fuel to the fire, shut the stove door and the window. This went on all day, with a sixty degree temperature change every hour. Each time she would demand to know why I was letting this happen. There I lay, too sick to even answer or defend myself.

I guess she was close to the answer to the age old question as how to cure a cold or the flu as I was better the next morning.

Although Aunt Rosa was of the old school, and she believed that children should be made to mind, she was good to us. Uncle Marvin enjoyed our little pranks and orneryness.

Aunt Rosa was a medium for one short period of her life and "talked with the dead" during this time. In the early part of this century many people believed in this, but I don't remember anything about it as I was too young, and no one told me anything. Many years later she told my wife the story.

At that time there was a famous medium named Amanda Blake, who lived in Ohio, across the river from Huntington, WV. People came from several states to see her and to try to communicate with the dead. Finally Aunt Rosa decided to go to see Amanda Blake to talk with an old friend who had died. The first thing Mrs. Blake said to her was, "Why are you coming to see me ? You can do the same thing. You have the gift the same as I do."

So Aunt Rosa bought a horn and started being a medium, and she said it worked. People came to see her from all over the county to contact their deceased friends or relatives.

My wife asked, "Why did you quit?" Her answer was that when she entered a room she felt that she was getting a request from somewhere, begging her to talk. Aunt Rosa was deeply religious, and she began to believe these were evil spirits calling her, so she threw the horn away.

My wife still feels that Aunt Rosa's horn would have been a great keepsake, and also that it might come in real handy when she found me listening to the radio, watching TV and reading a book at the same time. She wonders if she could use that horn to communicate with the dead--me.

RELATIVES

STEVE HARRISON

THE NUTTERS OF NUTTERVILLE
Hickory Flats, WV

The Nutter family in America has been traced back to Christopher Nutter in Maryland in 1637, where he was an Indian interpreter for the early Maryland government. There was a Nutter at Jamestown and another Nutter there soon after that. Whether they were the father and grandfather of Christopher Nutter we have not been able to prove, but we think they were even though we could not find any other Nutters in the area at that time. In England the Nutter family was so named because they were agriculturists in nut trees.

Christopher Nutter's descendants follow in Maryland records until about 1750, when our line moved to Sussex County, Delaware. Just before 1770 they migrated to Redstone, Pennsylvania, and then to near Clarksburg, WV, to a place stilled called Nutter's Fort.

Two Nutter brothers, Thomas and John, along with cousin Matthew (our ancestor) built the fort before the Revolutionary War. Matthew's son, David, was born in 1769. We have not found David's mother's name. Matthew's second marriage was to a Goodwin in 1775, and they had a large family.

David Nutter migrated to Monroe County and married Ruth Cottle in 1789, and they had ten children. She died in 1810 and is buried in the graveyard at the Rehobeth Church, the oldest Methodist church west of the Alleghenies.

David Nutter then migrated to Kessler's Cross Lanes in Nicholas County, in 1814, near where the Summersville Dam now is located. There he married Christina O'Dell, daughter of Jeremiah O'Dell, one of the first settlers in Nicholas County. David and Christina (O'Dell) Nutter were the parents of eight children. Their third child, John Nutter, was my great grandfather, and he married Elizabeth Pitzenbarger, daughter of Peter and Elizabeth (Amick) Pitzenbarger. They lived near what was later Nutterville. John and Elizabeth Nutter moved to Nutterville (Hickory Flats) just after 1850. John and two brothers camped in three protected hollows in open faced cabins along Hickory Flats, later called Nutterville, where they spent the winter clearing land and building cabins. John Nutter lived in a cabin with his family during most of the 1850's. My grandfather was born there in 1856. About 1850 John Nutter built a home and a huge log barn on the ridge. Part of the logs from the barn are still standing, but the house burned in 1980.

Hickory Flats (Nutterville) extended from just north of the Sugar Grove church and the fire tower south almost to Russellville, a distance of six miles. All of the farms and cleared land lay on top of ridges, much of it being flat land. Most of this country was owned by David and Christia Nutter's children. Several children of David's earlier marriage also came to this area. G.G., John and brothers owned the entire Hickory Flat Ridge. All of this branch of the family was fairly well educated for that time. They were knowledgeable, hard working farmers. Hickory Flats lay at the western end of Greenbrier County and extends into Nicholas County. My Grandfather Isaac married Mary Walker of near Nallen, across Meadow River in Fayette County. His father gave him land and an old schoolhouse where the Deitz farm and home now stand. Isaac Nutter built a new home there and established the first post office, which he named Nutterville. In about 1908 he sold the land to my parents and moved to his father's home (John Nutter). Here he lived until his death in 1936. This farm adjoined his old farm (my home) about one half mile north.

Alexander Nutter, who descended through David Nutter's first family, lived in a log house in Nutterville and was the father of a large family. Both he and his wife died in the late 1800's, leaving several married children, one daughter, Jemima, 12 years old, and three younger brothers. The four children decided to stay at home and raise themselves rather than to go to live with brothers and sisters. They raised a garden, canned, milked the cow and went to school.

Later Jemima married Emory (Bub) Flint and had several children, all of them living at the present time but one.

Jemima and one of these younger brothers continued to be our neighbors during my youth. The three boys were Joseph, John and Jasper.

MY NUTTER GRANDPARENTS

My grandfather bought a car in the old days when very few people knew much about the engines of cars, and this was especially true of my grandfather. He lived so far out in the country he didn't have anyone else to help him when the engine failed to start, so he would get out, raise the hood and look for a loose wire. Always the same routine would be followed. After about 30 minutes of looking, and he was getting madder and madder, Grandma would always ask, "Ike, could it be the engine?" Grandfather

Isaac Nutter, circa 1900

would throw his big black hat down on the ground and stomp on it.

Grandma developed a hearing problem as she got older, and about that time hearing aids began to be advertised, so Grandma and Grandfather had their son go buy one for her. He called to tell them the day he would bring it to her, and all of the children and grandchildren who lived near gathered to see this miracle. When this son arrived, the hearing aid turned out to be a big horn with batteries to be fastened to the belt. Everything was put in place, and instructions were read. The sound was turned on, and Grandfather said, "Mary, do you hear me?" She hadn't heard anything. Instructions were read again, and it was decided that the sound had been turned the wrong way, so it was turned the opposite way. Again Grandfather said real loud, "Mary, do you hear me?" Grandma then said, "Isaac, did I hear thunder?" Grandfather hit the floor laughing.

My mother's parents were very compatible, and they were good to us. They were completely different in one way: their sense of humor. Although Grandmother smiled a lot and laughed some, I never saw her laugh at something funny that happened or at a joke. Granddad loved jokes, pranks or funny incidents, and he loved to tease Grandmother, especially because of her inability to see through a joke.

Grandmother's father died just after the Civil War, leaving a wife and eight children, the oldest being thirteen. Grandmother was one of the oldest children. Soon after her father's death, their cabin burned, and nothing was saved: no clothing, no money, no tools, and no cooking utensils. Yet, her mother, being of the old pioneer stock, rebuilt her cabin with neighbors help. She raised the family, killed wild game, including a bear, skinned the bear and other game, raised gardens, and made do. It is no wonder Grandmother couldn't see a joke, for just surviving was hard.

Because she lacked a sense of humor, Grandmother was a great source of amusement to us "mean" grandchildren. She was always sweet and kind to us, but sometimes we just had to tell her some wild, ridiculous story that she couldn't catch on to, and we watched her completely serious, sober reaction to it. Grandfather loved this. One

Mary Walker Nutter, circa 1900

time she called our house on the telephone. My sisters were away at school, but one of them had come home for a visit. Grandmother was puzzled as to who was answering and asked, "Is this your mother?"

Grandfather was quite different from her in his reaction to funny happenings. If a person tried to pull a joke on him, he would have his work cut out for him. If the joke worked, he would love it and repeat the incident. One time my brother, Lawrence, stopped by their house, and Grandfather had a terrible cold. He told Lawrence about it and how he thought all of his brains were running out because of the way his nose was running. Lawrence consoled him and said that if that was his problem it wouldn't last long. That was Grandfather's favorite story, and he told it to everyone as long as he lived. Outsiders viewed him as a stern, all-business type of person, but the grandchildren never understood what they were talking about.

Although Grandfather grew up in a time when the woods were full of game, and the creeks were full of fish, he never hunted or fished and thought hunting and fishing were a waste of time. He would tell the grandsons about this, and, even though he meant it, he would tell it in a joking way. When I was the only one around to bring rabbits and squirrels in, he changed his mind and bought a gun. However, by this time, his eyesight was bad, and he had never learned to shoot and couldn't hit game at point blank range. He would try to shoot groundhogs but would miss. He was real disgusted as they were destroying his crops. My Father would tell him that it was no wonder he missed as he had put his gun past the target.

When it came time to butcher the hogs, he would have me shoot them, even though I was only ten or twelve years old. The older brothers were gone from home. He wouldn't even let the hired help shoot them. It had to be me. Having him call on me to do something he couldn't do was like winning a world championship.

Another thing he called on me to do was to catch his work horses from a twenty acre pasture field. He had caught them several times and would be mad and jerk on the halter straps and slap them. They got so they would keep walking away from him, and he would call for me. I could walk out into the pasture field without a bridle and walk up to the mare, Nellie, get hold of her mane, and climb on her back. Ned would follow her to the barn. I thought this was a great victory of some kind.

Granddad was really physically rough and tough. Although I never heard of him having a fight, he loved rough housing. He was stocky and strong, and Granddad's youngest son was a big, fast strong man. Granville was the same type. If Granddad caught them with their backs turned on the high porch, he would tackle them, and they would land a few feet below among Grandmother's tubs of asters and wrestle with them. When he was in his sixties and broke several ribs, he decided to quit having fun this way. I was too young to have gotten in on the rough housing.

One of my jobs was to ride the horse and guide it through the garden to cultivate or lay off rows for planting. The garden would be full of fruit trees, and he never could understand why a ten year old boy at ninety pounds wouldn't like to guide the horse straight into low limbs and get swept off into the plow or cultivator and not enjoy the pain. He would really describe how the younger generation was getting weaker but not any wiser. He was really having fun, not being serious, and if I came back with a good answer, it was even more fun for him.

He was a great teacher and fun to work with as he patiently explained why to do things one way instead of another. He never really bawled me out. One time I was carrying water to the field workers in a glass jug and dropped and broke the jug. I came in that evening and heard the hired lady telling him about it. Later I came to believe it was just to make her happy that he said it was my carelessness, that he didn't really care. That was the worst day of my life.

He was a very independent person, but he carried it too far sometimes. He had several strokes in the last years of his life, but at one point he was able to walk on crutches. One day he made his way down the road and had fallen into a fence corner and couldn't get up. My brother and I came by and were almost past him when one of us saw something out of the corner of an eye and discovered him. We helped him up and asked why he hadn't called out. He said if we didn't see him he just wasn't going to call us. He was just too proud.

Before he died when I was twenty, I came home and was told he probably wouldn't be able to communicate with me. However, he roused up and told me, among many other things, tha he had lain there many months wondering if he would ever see me again. I will never forget this. He would tell me and others that I was bright and intelligent. This always helped my self-confidence, coming from a source which I considered the final authority on knowledge.

Granddad was a great teacher in many ways. A cousin told me about Granddad instructing him how to cut potatoes for planting. He said, "Now don't look at two or three bushels at once. You just cut one potato at a time, and you slice it so that two eyes are left in each piece. Think of one potato at a time, and keep it simple."

This cousin, who was in the insurance business all of his adult life, said that when someone asked him to help them understand a policy, he would always use Granddad's advice and would look at one complicated clause at a time. He would get it reduced in his mind to a simple meaning and then go on to the next clause, thus reducing the meaning to something simple and understandable.

Granddad would teach more than farm work. He kept a large Webster's dictionary on a stand in the living room. He had been a school teacher earlier in life and highly educated himself beyond this. He would look up words he didn't understand and get the meaning. He was always asking the grandchildren meaning of words and explaining them or having us look them up. He might ask us again in a few days to see if we still remembered the word and meaning. After a few times we would doggone well remember, or we would have to listen to some great description of our lack of brain power.

Granddad's opportunities were so much greater than Grandmother's. His parents were the first settlers in that mountainous country of what is now Nicholas and Greenbrier Counties. As the land was cleared, it held rich soil until it was eroded through the years. Great-grandfather Nutter owned a lot of land, and he gave Granddad an uncleared farm when he married. He came from a tribe of people who were knowledgeable, hard working farmers who considered weeds, brush and filth in fence corners as personal enemies. Granddad inherited this outlook and won every skirmish and battle.

He got what was then considered a good education. His teacher during his boyhood was an Englishman, Mr. Blofeld, who had been well educated and had been Captain of the Queen's Guard, and was of English nobility, but he married a commoner and was then no longer royalty. He was given a land grant on what was supposed to be a navigable river in western Virginia. Was this ever wrong! He began to clear a mountain farm and teach school. After his English wife died, he married a Pitzenbarger, Granddad's aunt, and raised a large family.

Along with the Nutter cousins, Granddad was related to everyone in the western end of Greenbrier County: the

Amicks, the Pitzenbargers, the O'Dells, and the Williams families.

After Granddad finished grade school, the country school house was used to train teachers during the summer. Thus Granddad became a teacher and farmer. Later he became a surveyor and surveyed for fifty years for the Gauley Coal Land Co. He became prosperous by the standards of that area, with this steady income plus his farm. He became a bank director and was well known throughout the area.

An old man I worked with when I was young said when he was young Granddad used to pass their house and how impressed he was to see this man dressed in a black suit, a tie, black horse, black hat, and a black beard. He said he thought he was seeing General Grant. (You see, Johnny Cash wasn't the original man in black.)

Granddad used to have to board with farmers and hired help to clear brush in the line of sighting his compass. His favorite story was about boarding with a farmer who also helped him with surveying. This man was so soft spoken he could hardly be heard. After the man worked for Granddad a few days, Granddad started boarding at the man's house. The first time they sat down at his table, the man said the blessing. Instead of his soft voice, he suddenly boomed out the blessing in a voice that could be heard half a mile down the road, as though God was hard of hearing. Granddad was so startled he nearly jumped into the middle of the table.

Another time when his brothers were helping him survey a few miles from home, they stopped at a lady's home and asked to use her dining room table to eat as they had brought their lunch. This lady was an old friend of the oldest brother. While Granddad sat at one end of the table eating with the younger brother, the older brother sat at the side, talking over old times with the lady, who was sitting at the end facing all of them. Granddad finished lunch and started cutting a watermelon. The older brother was really startled when the lady, looking almost at him, suddenly said, "When you get through with that gentlemen I want his seeds."

There was another funny story Granddad liked to tell about an incident that happened in church. A neighbor of his got up to speak in church, and a hornet crawled up the man's pants leg and stung him. The man slapped his leg, killing the hornet, and said, "Damn that hornet," before continuing his talk without pausing.

He told of a senile Civil War veteran who was talking in church of his return from the war. He made a long talk, none of it logical. Granddad could repeat the entire talk, but all I remember was about the veteran telling how he was wading through the deep snow and came to a fence. Looking across it he described a beautiful field of ripe wheat.

MY SISTER AND THE LAW
BY LINDA DEITZ

Joyce was twenty years old when her husband taught her to drive. I, being exactly six years her junior, was at the age of fourteen terribly impressed with this major accomplishment.

She was living in North Carolina at the time this incident happened, and my parents and I went for a visit shortly after she acquired her license. It was late evening when we arrived, but my sister and I invented a reason to go to the store, which was several miles away. Since no one seemed anxious to join us, Joyce and I were off!

It was quite dark by this time, and the country road we were on was mostly deserted. We were driving slowly down the road, very pleased with ourselves, when suddenly a car pulled up behind us and turned on blinking red lights--a police car!

Joyce kept on driving, so I said, "Joyce, he wants you to pull over."

"He can't mean me. I'm only going thirty," she said, and kept on driving.

"Joyce, he must mean you. You're the only car on the road," I said. She couldn't argue with that logic and finally pulled over.

He parked behind us, and we waited for him to approach. Joyce rolled down the window and, in a panicky voice, said, "What have I done? What have I done?"

"Nothing, ma'am," he replied. "Your tail light is out."

We both heaved a sigh of relief until he asked to see her driver's license.

"Of course," she calmly replied, and then turned to me and said in a deadly whisper, "Get my driver's license." Luckily I had her pocketbook in my hands, so I pulled her billfold out and handed the license to her. She showed the policeman the license.

We thought our troubles were over, but worse was to come. "May I see your car registration", he asked in a reasonable voice.

"Just a minute," Joyce responded in the same tone.

109

Then she turned to me and hissed, "Find it!"

I had no idea what a car registration was and prayed that she did. I was rummaging through the glove compartment, hoping to find something that said "Car Registration" in neon lights when I realized my fervent prayers had been answered. Joyce had opened the car door, pointed to a piece of paper, and asked hopefully of the policeman, "Is that it?"

"No, ma'am," he replied, with a straight face. "That's your oil change sticker."

He told her to go home and ask her husband what a car registration was, but I'm sure she never did. She made me promise never to tell this story, and, of course, I never will.

JAYE AND THE CHRISTMAS SPIRIT

By Linda Deitz Good

When I was about 10 or 11, my older brother was working during the holiday season for our father at a Christmas tree lot. Since he was working after school and on weekends, he didn't have time to go shopping and asked me to do it for him. I agreed, and then we disagreed on the amount of money to be spent. I figured he was rolling in it, and he figured he wasn't. We went round and round; still I couldn't talk him out of parting with any more.

Finally, I had had enough, so, after he went to bed one night, I stated to the world what I thought of him. This must have worked, for early the next morning he gave Mom more money to give to me. When he had opened his door that morning he had found a sign stating, "Scrooge sleeps here."

110

NIKKISMS

Among the persons I have known who used mixed metaphors, substituted wrong words, said the wrong thing at the right time and did this innocently, our lovely daughter-in-law is one of the best (or worst) at this. When she and Jaye lived nearby I remembered many of these blunders and called them Nikkisms.

One time I stopped at their house, and their dog had gotten loose and now wanted in the house at the same time I got there. Nikki came to the door, opened it, and said "Come in stupid." She always said this wasn't a true Nikkism as she knew whom she was speaking to.

One time when my wife, Madeline, visited them in Panama in the Canal Zone, she was helping with dinner and had made the gravy. Jaye, our son, was fussing about the old shipped-in potatoes and how they tasted. Nikki advised him to put some of Mom's gravy on them as that would kill the taste of anything.

One evening, after picking up the youngest boy at the baby sitters, Nikki stopped by our house where our youngest daughter Linda was visiting. When Nikki started to leave, she went outside to call the youngest son, Alex. Here is Linda's version of the following Nikkism.

NIKKI - Linda Tells the Story

Down the steps went Nikki, George, and then me. Nikki was calling to Alex, the baby, and George was asking me to stop by their house. Nikki whirled around before I could reply and said in a firm voice, "George, I said NO - N-O, and I mean NO.

There was dead silence until Nikki started down the steps again. I said, in a quiet voice, "Maybe next time George."

Nikki whirled around again and asked me what he had asked in the first place. I said he had invited me to stop by

111

for a visit.

Nikki started laughing and explained she had thought George was asking to stop by the fire house to see Jaye, and she had already told him NO.

Nikki's laughter is infectious! You have to forgive her anything--even being un-invited to her house.

Where Nikki taught first grade one year, there were a lot of children from families on relief. Before Christmas that year she told the children: "Don't bring any present to me. I only want one present from all of you, and that is your good behavior." One little first grade boy came in with half a bottle of perfume unwrapped. In questioning him she found out that he had told his mother that if he didn't bring a present he would get a paddling. Nikki went to the office to call his Mother to explain exactly what she had said. She was embarrassed. Apparently she had found someone who could match her in what was said and what was meant to be said. When the conversation got so tangled that it was beyond salvaging, Nikki said goodbye' and hung up.

When Nikki turned around, the school secretary was staring at her bug-eyed. Nikki explained to her, "That's what my father-in-law calls Nikkisms. I'm always putting my mouth in my foot." she says she never tries to apologize for her apologies are worse than her Nikkisms.

When Nikki and Jaye moved to Panama in the Canal Zone, she started teaching first grade there. After a few days she stood talking with other teachers in the hall, and one of her students passed and didn't speak when she spoke to him. Nikki said, "What's the matter with the kindergarten teachers? Don't they teach them anything?" Of course, the teachers she was talking with happened to be kindergarten teachers. They put her on their list of "people we don't talk to" for about three months, but after that they began to accept and love her and her Nikkisms and could hardly wait to hear the next one.

Jaye worked in the fire department for a while here and would work 24 hours and be off 48 hours. He was a close friend to all the fellows on the police department, and because Nikki was afraid to be alone when he worked at night, he had her to leave a light burning in the living room, and he asked the boys on patrol to look for the light and to stop and check if it wasn't burning. This reassured her, and it was no trouble to the police patrol since Jaye lived on one of the main streets.

When Jaye took a job in the Canal Zone, Nikki stayed here for two months to finish her school year teaching and to sell the house. Nikki went to the police station to ask them to still watch the house. There was a well dressed, dignified looking man standing by the window when she went in and said to the man on the desk, "Ronnie, Jaye is out of town, and you know what the signal is." That man gave her a real shocked look.

Since they have moved I have not been able to collect many Nikkisms, although Nikki doesn't mind passing them on. Most of the time she just doesn't realize she has pulled one.

She did have one to share last summer. She and Jaye had gone to a party, and Nikki started talking to an official about a health hazard problem in school with the natives. She talked at length with one man. On the way home, Jaye asked her about the weird conversation she had been having, and which he had only partially overheard. Nikki said she thought Mr. Smith of the school system ought to know about the health hazard, and Jaye told her that was an official in the Marine Division. Jaye said, "I'll bet he thinks you have a real problem, taking up his whole evening talking about lice."

Nikki is a bright girl with a special talent.

I was at Jaye's and Nikki's house one time when George, the older boy, was three years old. Nikki never talked down to the boys, but more man to man, or woman to man. When George had a difference of opinion with her, he would sound like a lawyer, arguing his case very logically. That day he had something he wanted his mother to do, and Nikki was telling him no. He kept stating his case with great reason, so Nikki brought the discussion to a conclusion by telling him, "Now, George, as long as you live with us, eat our food and wear clothes we buy, you live by our orders, but if you want to go on your own, make your own living, then you can do as you want."

Nikki's favorite was not a real Nikkism, but since it was at my expense, she enjoyed it more than a Nikkism. In using the shower room at work I caught a real bad case of athlete's foot, or something similar, and doctors and specialists couldn't help me, even temporarily. One of my co-workers who had caught "jungle rot" while in service suggested medicine which had cured his case there. No doctor here had any idea what the medicine might have been. I had relatives in Panama, and they checked this out and got the name of a medicine which was available only at animal hospitals. I asked Nikki to pick this medicine up for me as she was going to stop at the animal hospital anyway. A girl filled the order and asked, "Is this for your dog or cat?" Nikki answered, "Oh, neither one, it's for my father-in-law." She still says, "Where else would you get medicine for a father-in-law?"

DEITZ GENEALOGY

The first Deitz who migrated to America was William Deitz, who came from the Lahr River, near Frankfort, Germany, in the late 1700's. He may have come through the Boston Port and then to Philadelphia, Pa., then he probably went down the Shenandoah Valley of Virginia. There is a Deitz castle still standing on the Lahr River in Germany. All Deitzes throughout the world trace back to this area or to the castle. One of the first of the Deitz name was supposed to have helped Martin Luther escape from his pursurers and was possibly hidden in the Deitz castle.

William Deitz married (Jane) Vacob (Wachob) in Virginia. They moved to Greenbrier County (now in West Virginia) and had twelve children, six boys and six girls. All West Virginia Deitzes seem to trace back to William Deitz, except those in the most northern West Virginia counties.

My line comes through the seventh child, John Deitz, who married Sarah Louisa McClung (1812-1866), who was the granddaughter of George Alderson (1762-1811) and Sarah Osborne. Sarah Osborne was the daughter of John Osborne (1730-1806) and Elizabeth Claypoole (1739-   ). Elizabeth Claypoole was the daughter of James Claypoole (1701-1789). This line will be traced by nearly 2,000 years.

Sarah Louisa McClung's father was James McClung (1770-1824), whose father was William McClung (1738-1833), a Revolutionary War soldier. His tombstone stands in the old Amwell cemetery in Greenbrier County. He was the first settler in western Greenbrier County and had a tomahawk claim on 100,000 acres, including the entire Meadow River basin. William's father was John McClung (1706-1788). William's wife was Abigail Dickinson.

Sarah Louisa McClung's mother was Mary Alderson (1787-1870). Mary was the daughter of George Alderson and Sarah Alderson mentioned above. George Alderson (1762-1811) was the son of Rev. John Alderson and Mary Carroll.

Rev. John Alderson was one of the earliest circuit riders

west of the Alleghenies. The town of Alderson, West Virginia, was named for him. Most of the early marriages in that area were performed and recorded by him. His father was also John Alderson, who migrated from England to New Jersey. His family was of high lineage, and his castle still stands in England.

My grandfather was Joseph Dickinson Deitz (1841-1919), apparently the Dickinson name being inherited from his Great Grandmother Abigail Dickinson McClung. He married Virginia Ellis (1840-1924), whose father was Jesse Ellis (1805-1874). Jesse Ellis' father was Jacob Ellis (1778-1856), who married Margaret Griffith on Nov. 17, 1798 in Greenbrier County (now West Virginia). Jacob Ellis' father was Owen Ellis, and his mother was Christina Van Dorn from New Jersey, or plain Dorn, in Virginia. Virginia Ellis' mother was Delilah Corron (1810-1887), the daughter of John G. Corron, who was the son of Robert Corron, a Revolutionary captain from Ireland. His mother was Lucy Pinnell (1773-184-), who was the daughter of James Pinell (1740-1820) and Elizabeth Wright.

To continue from James Claypoole, the genealogy is James Claypoole (1664-1706) who married Mary Cann. James Claypoole (1595-1664) married Mary Angell. Adam Claypoole (1565-1634) married Lady Dorothy Wingfield (-1619).

When my grandparents' oldest daughter was expecting her second child, my grandmother had a dream. In the dream a neighbor rode a brown horse to their house and delivered the news that the daughter, Matilda, had delivered the child, a little girl, but she wasn't expected to live. The next day this neighbor rode to the house, on a brown horse and delivered this exact bad news.

My grandmother hurried to see her, and Matilda died soon afterward. Before she died she told her mother never to ride across the bridge at Mt. Urim church.

From then on, grandmother would always get out of the buggy, walk across, and then get back in the buggy.

One time it was raining real hard. Grandfather told her to forget that foolishness, stay in the buggy, and not to get soaking wet.

She decided to follow his advice, but when the horses started onto the bridge, their harnesses started to rattle and jingle real loud. Grandmother jumped out of the buggy, walked across, and got back in the buggy. She never again tried to ride across the bridge.

116

FRIENDS &
CO-WORKERS

STEVE HARRISON

GEORGE

Maybe my all time favorite work buddy was George. I met George late in my working days, but then we worked together for a few years on the same crew and talked a lot about his experiences as a black man in a white world. One of my favorite stories he told was that after he had lived in this neighborhood for about 20 years a close neighbor came by and asked George to sign a petition. This neighbor was an old lady in her eighties, and George said, "Yes, Mrs. Jones, what is it?" Mrs. Jones said, "Haven't you heard? A black family is trying to buy a house down the street." George was a black man. Mrs. Jones was white and had forgotten he was black because she had known him so long. Mr. Jones would come over every couple of hours for a week or so to apologize. To George, this was a hilarious incident.

He loved to tell me about being black in a white world. Some stories were cruel, some sad and some funny. These were George's favorites. He held no grudges, no bitterness. He just told it like it was and was proud that, in spite of the roadblocks and handicaps, he had built his own home, educated his children, and had gone on low paying jobs until later years. The proudest accomplishment of his life was when his oldest daughter was graduated from college.

For many years George managed a parking lot. He told about two old maid sisters (white) who still drove without any confidence but would drive to town. First, they would call George to tell him to watch for them as they were coming to town. He would meet them in the street and park their car.

After their deaths, their brother, a lumber dealer, came to see George and talked with him several hours, asking a lot of innocent type questions. During the conversation he found out about George buying a lot and where and how he was buying a few blocks at a time and a few small loads of lumber when he could afford it. He worked (on the house) in his spare time.

A few days later, after hours, George went down to work

117

on the house, and on the lot were truck loads of material, enough to finish the house. George was really worried. He thought a supplier had misunderstood his small order, and he had no way to pay for it. He called all suppliers with no results and finally remembered that the brother of those old ladies was a supplier and called him. The brother said his sisters told him before their deaths to do something nice for George, so this was the answer.

George told me on one cold winter day he was in his building in the parking lot when he noticed a car across the street. There was a white couple with small children in the car. He kept seeing the father stop people who were passing and showing them something in his hand. Finally George got worried about the children in the cold and went over to inquire about the children. He discovered that the family was trying to sell a cigarette lighter for a dime to call home for money. George invited them over to his warm room on the parking lot. Before the mother from the deep South entered the building, she explained to George that he would have to stay outside. George, being George, explained the facts of life about that, so they entered the building, and George bought the children milk and snacks and gave the father the dime for a call for money. For many years the family would stop to see George, the mother always apologizing about her ignorance, having grown up in the deep South. She would say, "I just didn't know any better."

After George built his house, the neighborhood remained totally white for many years except for George. He looked on this as the land of opportunity for his sense of humor. Every time he did better with his lawn or garden or anything else, he would have his fun pouring it on about black superiority. One particular summer he reached the top of the hill. He planted an extra lot of tomatoes in his garden. The tomato blight hit all of his neighbors' tomatoes, but George had a bumper crop without blight. Naturally he gave them all tomatoes, but he made them pay in another way. He'd tell them that only blacks could get mother earth to respond, and whites couldn't raise anything. Finally they would say, "George, darn it, could you just leave the tomatoes on the front porch and let me pick them up, and you keep your mouth inside where I don't have to listen to it." That was his favorite summer.

For a few years, when jobs opened up in the automobile plants in Detroit, again he lived in a white neighborhood where, with a few exceptions, the people didn't even speak to each other. George, of course, started conversations with all of them. They would look at him as though they thought he was crazy, but before long they were showing him their lawns, gardens, flowers, boats and cars. After that they began to talk with each other, having neighborhood barbecues and get togethers. When he moved back to West Virginia they gave him a big party and told him that he had changed the whole neighborhood.

When I worked with George, most of us were white, and at breaks and lunch hour we would bring up something to inspire George to pour it on. He was absolutely the best at repartee I ever saw. The starting remark could be anything, even racial, and George could care less, as if he didn't have a prejudiced or resentful bone in his body. He seized these golden opportunities with absolute delight, and, as the old saying goes, he would have them rolling in the aisles.

I used to tell George I would actually bite my tongue off before I would let him know that he had gotten under my skin. He was totally inspired to go on if he knew he was getting to you with his fun--he was at his best at this. After I retired George had a heart attack and died on the job. He was the best loved and most missed among his co-workers of anyone I ever worked with.

It still gives me a sad feeling to visit the plant, knowing that George is not there to greet me.

DUCK

I first met Duck when he came to work in the Tech Center store room, but I remembered when he played basketball and baseball at South Charleston High School. He had a brother, Paul, who had been a great basketball star at South Charleston and later at Marshall College. He got the name Duck because he walked and ran with a waddle like a duck.

Our first conversations started because our son, Jaye, was playing basketball at South Charleston High School, and Duck was a basketball fan and player. He had been in service and graduated with one of the neighbor boys, who was always playing ball with our son in the street. Our son was only about 12 years old when the neighbor boy entered service. The neighbor boy, Joe Ranson, began to tell Duck about this little ball handling guard and what a whiz he was--what a prospect he was. After four years, Duck got out of service and just had to see this basketball whiz for himself, so he went to a B team game, as Jaye was just then a high school sophomore.

Duck watched the team warm up, but he couldn't pick out anyone to fit Joe's description of a little ball handling, play-making guard, so he asked someone which one was Jaye. The boy who was pointed out had grown to six feet four and 145 pounds, all bone, and with a loose awkward look, as though he was always about to fall on his face. Duck was disgusted, but he stayed to see if Jaye could make it up the court without falling. From that game on, Duck was one of Jaye's greatest fans, for Jaye just didn't play like he looked.

Later, when Jaye played at West Virginia University, Duck, his wife, little boy, my wife, our daughter and I went to Morgantown to see a game. Duck loved to argue and kid people, and my wife is the type of person who seems to be teased by almost everyone, so we had hardly gotten on the road before they started a fun feud that lasted for years. My wife, Madeline, happened to tell of an incident that took place a few days before when she had found an oily-looking part lying under our car. She took it to Mr. Harrah at the garage, who said it was nothing from the car. He laughed and told her to think nothing of it as a lady a few weeks before had run over a manhole cover, had some way wrestled it into her car, and brought it into the garage for him to replace on her car.

Duck immediately attributed the incident to Madeline and would tell the story to everyone.

At Morgantown we stayed with Duck's parents. His father, a minister, refused to let us pay for staying or for the great food his wife prepared. Their church had some little banks they were selling for fund raising, and, since we couldn't pay them, I filled one of the little banks with money. I bought some of the banks to take home, and later Duck's wife discovered Duck had picked up the bank with the money in it. My wife always accused Duck of stealing the church money.

When we let Duck and his family off at his home, he told us how much he enjoyed being with our daughter and me, purposely leaving Madeline's name out, but she got even many times.

As long as I worked around Duck I served as conduit for their insults and jokes. I would tell each of them anything funny that happened to the other, and then I would carry the remarks of the other one back. Duck's favorite was of an incident concerning one of her quick replies to me. I usually got home within a minute or two of the same time each day. One day I unlocked the front door and found her using a vacuum sweeper, with her back turned, so she didn't hear me enter. I put my arms around her, and, without turning, she asked, "Who is it?"

Duck was a real good soft ball player. Sometimes I would stop by to see him play, and he would come over between innings and start telling his teammates how sorry he was for me and what a terrible situation I had married into. Then I would go home and tell Madeline the latest story Duck had made up about her. She would enjoy his imagination and always sent back an appropriate reply.

I went to work in another area, and one of my new fellow workers met Duck at a ball game. This person told me later that Duck started telling him how sorry he felt for me--what a horrible choice I had made in marriage, etc. This man was really shocked I hadn't mentioned any problems. Duck finally explained that this was his favorite joke.

Duck and Madeline finally agreed to call the feud a draw after twenty years.

Duck told me of a funny incident at a football game. He was sitting behind a well dressed man, and there was a woman sitting beside him with a four or five year old girl. The little girl was a terror. She would run past this man, stepping on his feet, putting dirty hands on his clean coat, and spilling soft drinks on him. The man never said a word, and the mother never corrected the child. Finally, at half time, the man bought hot coffee and was drinking it. The child flung an arm out, spilling the hot coffee all over his lap. This time the mother offered a half apology, and the man answered, in a real kind voice, "Oh, that's all right, being that the poor little thing is retarded." The mother was very indignent and said the child wasn't retarded. The man stuck with his guns, still in a quiet voice, saying that he was sure she was, and he suggested that the mother should take the child to a doctor. The mother grabbed the child by the arm and left in a huff, allowing the man to watch the balance of the game in peace.

Duck loved to argue and get someone upset. He was willing to take the opposite side of anything anyone mentioned, including politics, religion, baseball, basketball or football. Someone might come to the window of the store room and Duck would seem to be in a heated argument. A few minutes later you might hear him in an equally big argument on the opposite side, using the argument the first person used on him. Even though he had serious beliefs, he was willing to argue the opposite side in order to get the person to argue with him. One time I walked up to the window for something, and Duck was arguing politics with someone who was backing Ted Kennedy. Naturally, Duck was arguing for Nixon, and he told the man, "Now look, Nixon got a man on the moon, and Kennedy couldn't get a sick girl across a bridge."

Duck like to tease a buddy, Kenny, who was good natured, hardly ever got upset, and enjoyed the funny things Duck would say to him. Kenny always drove to work with his wife and got out. His wife, Hazel, would get out and walk around the car to the driver's side and drive a few miles to where she worked. Although Duck hadn't met her at that time, he happened to be close by when she walked around the car, and he suggested that she not drop her troubles off on us. She looked puzzled and drove off to work. Kenny reported the next morning that Hazel had driven on to work, trying to figure out what Duck had meant. When the meaning hit her, she nearly wrecked the car she was laughing so hard. She had a great sense of humor, and she used this expression for years when she left Kenny off somewhere.

Every summer Kenny and his brothers went to Canada to go fishing for a week. While he was gone, Duck would fix up a card and have all the boys Kenny worked with sign it and mail it to Hazel. The card would say, "Hope you are enjoying Kenny's vacation as much as we are."

Finally Duck got under Kenny's skin, and he got even. One lunch hour, in front of several people, Duck really got going good about fisherman, and Kenny in particular. He said the dumbest people in the world could catch fish, that the laziest people could catch fish, that was what therapists used to calm down people with mental problems. This time Kenny was really mad. He left in a huff, with tool belt jangling and clanging at his side. He slammed the door as he went out. Duck had everyone laughing when Kenny came marching back through the door. He walked up to Duck, looked him in the eye and said, "I passed an insane asylum last week and do you know what the patients were doing?" Duck asked what they were doing, and Kenny said, "Playing ball." Duck, of course, loved to play ball, but he still likes to tell how Kenny got even at one try.

Duck's favorite story of getting ahead of my wife, Madeline, was about when we stopped by to watch Duck play softball. He was playing and managing the team, too. Between innings he came over to talk to us about the headaches of managing. He was telling her about how he hated choosing one player over another and maybe not being able to substitute because of closeness of the game. He told how two players might almost be equal and both would be his good friends. Madeline sympathized with him and said she realized that it would be a difficult decision. She added some philosophy, saying sometimes a decision just had to be made, and like Harry Truman said, if you couldn't stand the heat, stay out of the kitchen. The

123

discussion was serious for them, but then it stopped. Duck told her that he could understand her viewpoint, but he was warm hearted and of a sympathetic nature and was bothered by these things. He said he was sure he could understand how she would be able to handle the same situation with a cold hearted, hard headed way without regret.

Duck loved his reply and is still as proud of it as an old mountaineer who had first learned how to make corn whiskey.

Duck liked to tell of the time he was put down pretty good. Two of the boys came to the store room window for supplies, and one of them said to the other one, "You know, Duck was right about what we were arguing with him about yesterday. I looked it up." Behind him was an old buddy of ours, Johnny Childers. Johnny said to them, "Don't feel bad. Anyone who talks as much as Duck just has to be right once in a while."

There was one other story I told Duck about my wife. She had a fun feud with Red at the service station where we bought gasoline for about thirty years. She had gone to school with Red. When she would come by to purchase gas or to have the car worked on, he would swear that his whole day would be ruined by her appearance. She could always get even and maybe ahead by his workers tipping her off any time Red pulled a boo-boo, and she would give him a hard time about it. One day she came in and asked him if five gallons of gasoline would last her until payday. He really told her off, asking, "How in the heck would I know how far you are going to drive?" Duck would, of course, accuse her of being just that dumb.

SMITTY

Of all the people I ever worked with, Smitty was probably the wildest. He was borrowed from the Carbide Institute plant when our work load got heavy and stayed heavy, and worked mostly with me for five or six years. Smitty was a good worker, always doing his share, and there was never a dull moment around him. He and his wife had three young boys, and he had built his own home. As time went on, he began to have a drinking problem and grew more irresponsible. Sometimes he failed to get home with a full pay check. I used to tell him that I didn't know how in the world his wife could raise four little boys (Smitty being the fourth). If he had a few extra dollars after pay day, and his wife needed a few dollars, he would be broke. He loved to use one of the fellows named Bob as his excuse for being broke. She didn't know the man at that time, and, since this man was a teetotaler and a square (according to Smitty's life style), Smitty thought it was the funniest joke in the world to tell her that Bob had borrowed money for whiskey, beer or to play cards. He might tell her the exact truth about where the money had gone but name the wrong person who had spent it.

He and his wife were riding in the car one day when he had to suddenly hit the brakes, and a partially filled bottle of whiskey came sliding from under the seat, slowly across the car floor and stopped between her feet. Before she could say anything, Smitty said, "That Bob borrowed my car today and went to the liquor store, and, darn him, he's left a bottle in the car." Finally, when she threatened to go to his boss and get him transferred back, he had to confess as he liked to work on the hill. Every once in a while he would mention the whiskey bottle incident and always say, "That was the fastest thinking I ever done in my life."

Smitty loved to argue with everyone, and he was an agitator. People would threaten him, give him the dickens and argue with him but never get mad at him because the things he would do and say were so funny and harmless.

Someone might tell a story or experience, and Smitty would take the story and, with his great imagination, would tell the story back to or in front of the person with his additions.

One good natured fellow, who worked in the same building with us, told us some of his experiences around Smitty. Smitty called this man Wilmer because of some story he told us, and Smitty made his own additions, but I don't remember the story. I mean I don't remember the original story. I do remember Wilmer would tell Smitty a story, and then Smitty would tell it back to someone in front of Wilmer. I have seen Wilmer laugh until tears ran down his cheeks when he listened to Smitty's version. Wilmer would never deny Smitty's version but would go along with Smitty's story as being the original version.

One of the stories was that a neighbor of Wilmer's had gone to the hospital, so Wilmer went over to mow the neighbor's lawn. While he was mowing, the neighbor's wife came out in the yard. She was wearing a brief halter and shorts. Wilmer was mowing and watching the wife at the same time, and he mowed down some shrubs and roses. When someone asked Wilmer why he was so careless, he replied, "Huh, you just try to mow north while you are looking south sometime."

Another time Wilmer told of growing up during the depression in the mountains above Williams River in Webster County. Things were real bad, and then, to add to their troubles, Wilmer's father loved to trade, and when a horse trader came by and wanted to trade, his father, not having a horse to trade, traded all of their 90 chickens for a mule while the family was away. The next day the mule died, and they lived on boiled cabbage for the next four years of the depression.

Wilmer joined the circus when he was about seventeen and traveled all over the country. The circus made a stop at the Greenbrier County fair at Lewisburg. Wilmer was in his sleeping tent one night and, while drinking a few beers and smoking, he set his tent on fire, and the whole circus burned. It was obvious where the fire had started, Wilmer thought, so he took off and hitch hiked rides toward the Williams River. Then he hitch hiked west along Route 60, then north toward Richwood. When he started north from Route 60 he could hear the police sirens going on west looking for him. That was the end of his circus career.

A friend of mine, Bill, worked from the same building,

looking after chemical storage, inventory and ordering. Smitty loved to enlarge on Bill's experiences and stories and "get on his case." Bill enjoyed Smitty's imagination and trying to get under his skin. One bitterly cold winter day the antifreeze boiled out in Smitty's car. He filled it with water, drove to work and drained the radiator. He went to Bill and told him about his problem and how he needed antifreeze. Bill, being in charge of supplies, had had a problem with an antifreeze shortage due to it being used in the sudden cold weather. Since he felt sorry for Smitty, and he liked Smitty, he finally located a drum of antifreeze. He finally got it on a rack, opened it, and gave some to Smitty. Smitty then told Bill, pointing to his throat, "Bill, I'm all choked up to here being good to you until I get this dog gone antifreeze." Bill still laughs about this.

Smitty started missing work more often as time went on, and when the boys would inquire where he had been, he would have all kinds of answers, including that he had spent the day at their house. They mostly asked him in order to hear these funny replies so they could laugh at him. Nothing the boys would reply bothered him in the least, except for me, for some peculair reason. We got along really well. This was easy for me as he talked and kidded so much that I finally could anticipate the things he was apt to say. I could just lay back and laugh at his getting on me, until sooner or later he would make the perfect remark for an answer.

One time he missed work on Monday, and later in the week when we were working on a rush job with several other fellows, someone asked him where he had been on Monday. He replied that he had visited at my house. I snapped my fingers and said, "That explains something that has puzzled me all week." Smitty asked what it was. I said, "Well, when I went home Monday evening my wife grabbed me around the neck, hugged me and said, "it's sure good to have a man in the house." The boys couldn't believe that Smitty could be left speechless for an answer.

127

SALESMAN CLINK
STORY BY A FELLOW WORKER

At one time I worked in a hardware wholesale and retail store in Virginia. Mr. Clink worked with me on Saturdays in the retail store, but through the week he traveled and sold farm machinery to the farmers in southwest Virginia. Some great stories came back from his customers. He would sell a piece of equipment or farm machinery to a customer with promises of extra attachments that he would throw in with the purchase. These customers would start coming in or sending word about not receiving the extra promised attachments; in fact, just raising cane about the situation and promises. Mr. Clink would call on them again, and this would give the customer a chance to personally tell him off about his promises. He would totally ignore their complaints, as though he didn't hear a word they were saying. At the same time he would be telling them about a great new piece of equipment which they just had to have in order to operate the farm, again promising extra attachments which he would throw in with the purchase. He would always end up selling the new piece of equipment, and the whole deal would be repeated. Several months of complaints followed about again not receiving the attachments, and then he would call on them again. Again he would ignore their complaints and get another order.

One Saturday a farmer came in to purchase a new wagon tongue, bringing with him an old wagon tongue he had hewn out of a hickory sapling to use temporarily when his wagon tongue had broken. He had brought it along to make sure the new wagon tongue was the same size. Mr. Clink insisted that we should not throw the old wagon tongue away, and we made a lot of comments about him having the place cluttered up with this old piece of junk.

One Saturday a customer came in, looking for this size wagon tongue, and I happened to be standing by and overheard his sales talk. He explained that he would sell a new wagon tongue for about $35.00 and then said, "Now I can let you have a Virginia hand hewn wagon tongue for $10.00, and he sold the old, twisted hickory wagon tongue."

128

Mr. Clink was noted for his driving habits. He would get to studying about a sales pitch he was going to make and forget to take his foot off the gas pedal. I had some hairy rides about eight miles on Saturday over a crooked, paved mountain road. One day, after the company had bought him a new ford pickup truck, he headed over the crooked mountain road, hitting the turns at full speed. At one of the worst hair pin turns the truck wheels on one side seemed to lift off the road, and I was sure we were about ready to roll down the mountain, Mr. Clink remarked casually, "You just can't beat these fords on mountain roads."

His son told about riding with him up Route 11 toward Roanoke at about 85 miles per hour when he passed two cars. The first car then passed the second one and turned on a siren. He stopped, and a state policeman came up to the car and said, "You are the darndest man I ever saw. Here I am chasing a speeder, and you pass both of us.

One time Mr. Clink stayed all night with one of his customers, a wealthy farmer who liked to drink. One morning Mr. Clink got up early and went to the front porch, which faced a beautiful 25 acre field. The farmer came out and offered him a drink of moonshine, but Mr. Clink explained he didn't drink. The farmer replied, "My gosh, if all of the moonshine I've drunk was on that field, I'm satisfied that it would be too wet to plow."

MAC

For several years I worked with Mac as a chemical worker. Sometimes we worked together, and sometimes I relieved him. At other times he relieved me on shift. He was great fun to work with as he had a great sense of humor. He remembered all the jokes he had ever heard and all the funny incidents that ever happened to him or his family, and he would tell everyone about them. He had several brothers and had at least one or more stories about each of them. Since Mac lived several miles away, and the brothers worked elsewhere, we only knew them by Mac's stories and his nicknames for them, such as the lightning brother, the moonshine brother, etc. I don't remember how all of them got nicknames except for the dynamiting brother, and that story I remember well.

One evening when Mac relieved me on day shift, he came in very serious and upset and told me about a near tragedy in the family that had just happened. It seems that one brother had just moved into a new house he had built, but he still needed a ditch dug for a pipe line for gas. Since the younger brother had just returned from service and needed work, he agreed to dig the ditch, with the help of a couple of buddies. After digging for some time across a field, they came to large imbedded rock that they couldn't break up. After discussing the problem, the younger brother remembered seeing dynamite in the basement, so they thought they could blow the rock out. They placed several sticks of dynamite on top of the rock and packed dirt around it. Then they placed a huge rock on top. (They definitely were not specialists.) Then they lit the fuse with enough length to allow them to get behind something and be in the clear. When the dynamite went off, the large rock went sky high, completely out of sight. After a little while they spotted a speck in the sky which got larger and larger. They realized that the rock was heading for the new house. This really scared them as the mother-in-law and her two sisters were in the house.

Sure enough, the rock hit the comb of the roof, came through the second floor, the first floor and landed in the basement. The boys rushed into the house and found the three elderly sisters all in one rocking chair, but unhurt. When I found out no one was hurt, I really cracked up.

Mac is probably telling this story thirty five years later and still referring to his younger brother as the dynamiting brother.

Mac loved fast cars and always drove a new Mercury with a straight stick. One morning when I relieved him he told me very seriously that he had to take his Mercury to the garage because it seemed to have a slight shimmy above ninety miles per hour.

One midnight shift when he and his car pool of riders came to a stop light at Spring Hill, there beside was a Cadillac with a girl driver who kept easing forward, ready to beat him away from the light when it changed. Mac accepted the challenge. He told his riders, "Watch me burn that caddy away from the light." When the light changed, the Cadillac jumped forward, but Mac's Mercury leaped backward, the steering wheel hitting him in the chest. One of his riders had slipped it in reverse. Mac's sense of humor deserted him that time, and he never forgave those men. He would say years later that they were still denying slipping it into reverse, but he said he knew darn well they did because they were all braced.

One time I filled in for Mac on his regular shift while he took a week's vacation to plant a garden. Before going to work on the midnight shift, we had a habit of going early and stopping at the triangle restaurant to drink coffee and shoot the breeze. Some one asked where Mac was, and I said he was on vacation. He then asked where Mac had gone. Like a lot of us in those days, I was addicted to taking a small fact and making up a ridiculous story that wasn't supposed to be believed. Maybe then some one else would add something even more ridiculous just for entertainment. I said Mac was farming, and some one asked if he had a farm. I said, "Not really, but he is planting eleven acres of lettuce."

The fellow asked, "What in the world is he going to do with eleven acres of lettuce?"

"Oh," I said, "Mac really likes lettuce and eats a lot of it."

A week or so later Mac was back at work with me and took some samples to the lab. When he went to the lab, one of the fellows said to his co-worker, "Here's that fellow that planted eleven acres of lettuce." Mac chuckled for years that I had made someone believe such an unbelievable story.

Once Mac finished the three to eleven shift and went out with the boys and didn't get in until the next morning after daylight. He had just sold his house and had a new one built. It was finished except for the living room, which still needed to be plastered. Many bags of plaster were stacked a few feet from the back wall opposite the front door. When he finally got home and tried to open it, his wife had locked him out. Mac said, "I backed up about fifteen feet, gathered up all my muscles, and said to myself that I'll just bust it down." About the time he hit the door, Millie opened the door. He couldn't stop, hit the plaster sacks, went over the top, got knocked out, and Millie let him lie there and get his day's sleep.

Mac resigned from the plant and went to work for a chemical plant in Florida, and we weren't in touch very often for about 25 years. Finally we got to visit for a few hours, and he asked me about an incident I had told him about when we worked together but I had forgotten about. The incident happened when I was in high school.

A group of fellows I knew went trout fishing back in the mountains around Cold Knob every spring and camped out for a week or two. This particular year they camped in an open spot on the opposite side of Clear Creek from a house where a mountain woman lived with several pretty daughters.

Back then, in those isolated hollows, people might use or pronounce words entirely different from people a few miles away. Anyway, the fisherman noticed a lot of winter onions growing in the garden of this family. One of the fellows went to the house and asked the mother about buying some onions. She looked at him and said they didn't have anything like that. The fellow tactfully pointed to the garden and said that was what he wanted to buy. The mountain woman then said, "Oh, you mean yengins. You people talk so funny. You know last week some people were camping in the same spot fishing. One of them came over and wanted to buy poontang. If I had knowed what he was talking about, we might have had plenty of it."

Mac said he had told that story a thousand times and had

132

gotten a thousand laughs out of it.

Mac loved his little pranks as well as his joke telling. Everyone in the building kept cokes in our cooler, including two or three girls. Some of them hated to get their cokes at noon when Mac was on the day shift because of his pranks. To identify the cokes, everyone would put his or her initial on the cap. Once in a while Mac would take an empty coke bottle, fill it with cold coffee, recap it and put someone's initial on it. Often the person would open the bottle there and take a drink and then spit iced coffee all the way across the room.

One noon hour one of the girls came in, got her coke and paused to talk a minute. Mac happened to be directly behind her and asked her something which she only partially heard. She turned around and asked, "Mac, did you want me?" Mac said, "Of course I want you, but my wife is so narrow minded she would never let me bring you home."

Once he called one of the girls across the hall on the phone after putting cheesecloth over the speaker. He said, "This is the telephone repairman, would you leave the telephone off the hook a few minutes while I blow the line out?" The girl was busy and laid the phone down without giving it a thought. Mac then went across the hall and put a handful of sand in front of the receiver and asked another girl to ask why the telephone was off the hook. Ella Mae began answering and analyzing the request at the same time. She said, "The telephone man called and, and (spotting the sand in front of the receiver)," she said, "Oh, my gosh." She received calls for a week to blow the telephone line out.

There were some cabins a few miles away from us that were famous for two hour rentals. There was a gas explosion in one of the cabins, and some of the occupants were hurt. The story was in the newspapers. As the girls would come by to get their soft drinks, Mac would be real sympathetic and inquire if they had been scared or hurt in the explosion. By that time they knew what to expect of Mac and just laughed at him.

Our department head, Bob, loved Mac's jokes, but he could never remember them when he tried to retell them. Knowing this, Mac would always save jokes for his 3 to 11 shift so he could tell Bob a joke. At exactly five o'clock the

133

phone would ring, and it would be Bob asking, "Mac, how did that joke go?" Bob would get home and try to tell the joke to his wife and have to call Mac for the punch line.

Bob's assistant was JB, who would only check on the unit one weekend a month. The rest of the time he worked in a larger unit. He was a nice person, but he was terribly absent minded when he was thinking about something. When Mac would be on day shift on Saturday he would watch for JB, and when he saw him park and get out of his car with a far away look in his eyes, Mac would station himself in the doorway. JB would turn sideways, squeeze past Mac without seeing him and go read the shift notes. Then he might stop and talk for an hour. Mac loved it when this would happen and chuckle all week about it.

JB got a dent in his car fender once and asked Bob to go up town with him for an estimate. Bob's story was that they drove up town to the garage, and JB got the manager to give him an estimate. Without a word, JB got back in his car with Bob, drove several blocks absently, and suddenly said, "Thank you." This was a favorite of Mac's.

Another incident concerning Mac and his new fast cars occurred when he was driving home from work at high speed. A state policeman stopped him to give him a speeding ticket, and the policeman turned out to be an old acquaintance. When he came to the driver's side of the car, Mac got out of his car and raised his hands high in the air. Both of them were well known in the area, and the policeman was the one who was embarrassed. Mac could not have cared less. The picture was that here was a policeman having a solid citizen stopped with his hands in the air. Cars were slowing up and even stopping, wondering what kind of serious crime had taken place. The policeman kept saying, "Get your hands down, get your hands down, Mac." Mac kept them high in the air. Finally the policeman said, "Get the h--- back in the car and get out of here. Forget the darn ticket. Just get going."

There was another funny story involving a policeman which Mac told. He was driving through Milton with his ten year old boy in the backseat, and he went through a red traffic light. On down the road the town policeman stopped him and told him he had run a red light. Mac got out of the car and said, "No, I don't think that light was red when I went through it." Little John, from the back seat, piped

up and said, "Oh, yes, Daddy, it was red."
Mac was really fun to work with.

OUR NEIGHBOR, HENRY

Although I refer to Henry as a neighbor, he actually lived a few miles away, but we used to know him fairly well as we fished and hunted in that area, even though it was a remote area. We also had relatives who lived beyond him, and we visited with them often.

Henry lived on a farm in an isolated region, almost two miles from his nearest neighbor. He was a pious, church going, honest, well liked man. He was the delight of the whole area because of his ability to say the wrong thing, causing it to sound ridiculous or hilarious. Most of his well circulated misstatements occurred in church meetings, where he would give testimonials. These things must have been true because of the number of people who heard or witnessed them, and they would be repeated time and time again around the country.

Most of the stories I used to hear about Henry had happened when he was older, and by that time the older children in the family were gone, leaving Henry, his wife and an unmarried daughter at home. According to visitors, some of their conversations were unforgettable.

They might start discussing an event of forty or fifty years before, and Henry would start out, "It was Saturday about eleven o'clock," when a voice from the kitchen would say, "No, Dad, it was nearer to twelve o'clock. Don't you remember Bill Cole went to mill that day and passed a little before eleven o'clock." The daughter wasn't born at that time, but she would recognize what Henry was about to tell and correct him to get the time exact. Usually the exact date would be told with corrections from the kitchen or some other room.

Bud Cole had once been the nearest neighbor and would pass their place on his way out. It was often said that Henry used B.C. to mean Bud Cole, not Before Christ.

An exact date, time of day, the hour and weather were given with each story, along with the daughter's corrections.

One visitor told of stopping by, and Henry was not there, but his wife and daughter were eating breakfast. It was a mistake to ask the wife how she was, for she had enjoyed a life time of bad health, and her answers were as detailed as a medical book, with every pain of several years being retold and enjoyed again in the telling. The wife sat there, eating a huge breakfast of ham, eggs, potatoes, pancakes and syrup, while she told him about her diet. She said the doctor put her on a diet of only wild game and fresh caught fish, along with just a few other limited numbers of fruit and vegetables. The visitor wondered if the diet was eaten before or after these main meals.

Henry's ability to say or tell something totally funny while being serious was unbelievable. He never knew that he had said something with an entirely different meaning from what his thoughts were. My uncle told of meeting Henry and asking about a forest fire in the area. Henry said, "Well, the first I knew about it was that John and Minnie stayed all night here. They had gone to bed, and a little while later John smelled a little smoke in bed."

My uncle could hardly keep a straight face, so he quickly changed the subject by asking about Henry's wife's sister, Hetty. Henry answered, "You know Hetty is staying with and caring for her parents. I've just got to go see her. Do you know that she hasn't been with a man for six months." My uncle never did figure out what straight-laced, church going Henry was actually trying to say.

Henry's biggest bloopers were in church when he was testifying before the entire congregation. One time Mrs. Jones testified that she felt so unworthy and so inferior to her fellow church members that she really shouldn't be among them, but should be hiding behind the church door. Henry arose and told that he, too, was unworthy to be among the more upright members and was ashamed that he didn't measure up to their high standards in any way. Therefore, he felt it to be only right that he, too, should be behind the door with Sister Jones.

After riding two or three miles to attend church, at one meeting he testified about his ride to church and of a place along a lonely road where a large tree had fallen, leaving a high root wall beside the road. He said it was his habit to stop at this root and pray, especially if anything was bothering him. He continued, "This morning, as I rode to services, I felt especially weak and unworthy, and I felt I just did not measure up to the rest of you, so when I got to this place, I got off my horse and grabbed my root and prayed."

Another Sunday Henry described his ride to church that morning, and he said as he rode along he felt sad when comparing himself with his fellow church members. They were so strong, and he was so weak. As he passed that tree it occured to him that right there was a perfect comparison between him and his brothers and sisters. He said. "There stands a mighty oak, strong and solid, resisting the blowing winds, with leaves bright and alive. That oak tree represents my friends, strong and solid in their faith, their spirits bright and alive. Then I saw nearby a worm eaten beech tree, knotty and with holes and hollows at the butt. I say that's Henry, that's ME."

One meeting day he stood up in front and told anyone who wanted to go to heaven to just come up front and shake his hand. The next Sunday the minister in his sermon made it sound as though it just wasn't that simple.

At another time Henry got up to make an announcement about the ice cream social the church was having. Members were to donate the ingredients, and Henry said, "All you women who give milk be here at two o'clock."

Henry was fairly articulate and wasn't noted for mixing up his words to any great degree--he just mixed up the meanings. One time he managed to do both. The congregation was to elect a new Sunday School Superintendent and an adult class teacher. Henry was mentioned for both positions, and he made the following announcement so the congregation would know his position in either case. He wanted to make it clear that, if elected, he would always try to be there, regardless of the long ride, through rain or snow or sleet, but, if he wasn't elected, he would not try to make it at times through the mud and bad weather. His words were, "If you elect me as Superintendent or as teacher of the adultery class, I will always make it. If not, I probably won't be here too often."

Henry didn't confine these bloopers to church. He just had a large audience who remembered and repeated them. He said these things almost every day.

Henry brought to town large amounts of farm produce, fruit, eggs and butter in his wagon, and his customers had many stories to tell about his mixed up meanings. One lady asked him if his hens were producing many eggs, and he told her they were producing well except for one day when his son, Junior, was visiting home, and they had not laid one egg that day. The lady wondered why the hens were mad at Junior.

Another customer asked Henry why he was later than usual on his rounds, and Henry explained that when he got up that morning one of his cows was feeling romantic, so he had taken her to see her boy friend.

One day Henry was talking to a neighbor and telling him why his wife had not gone to church the previous day. He said his wife had poor circulation in one leg and could not go to church due to the long, cold ride. When he came home they went to bed, where he held her leg between his. He told her about the church meeting and how they lay and meditated and were both satisfied. Henry left some of the details out, making the story much more lurid than the neighbor's interpretation.

No one ever accused Henry of ever being anything but pious and straight laced, or who would purposely say an off-color word. Henry succeeded without meaning to.

Although the neighbors saw through Henry's meanings, he usually left the listeners with at least two interpretations of what he had said. If his mixed-up stories had been kept (and not forgotten), several volumes could be written about Henry's bloopers.

MY FRIEND, EDDIE

When I boarded in town to go to high school, I used to stop at a little restaurant, where I made friends with the proprietor, Eddie. Eddie used to tell me stories about himself.

He said he left home at eleven or twelve years old and got a job in West Virginia as helper to the log camp cook, which gave him board and a few dollars for clothes until he got old enough to go to work cutting timber and later as a coal miner. He had never gone to school and was illiterate, but he still got to be a successful restaurant owner.

After being gone eight or ten years, he went back home for a visit. The family had not heard from him as he couldn't write. As he made his way home to a little crossroads by train and started walking towards home, a distance of two or three miles, he overtook an eight year old boy carrying a gallon can of kerosene. In asking the boy questions, he found that this was his kid brother, born after he left home, so he asked the boy about his brother Eddie (himself). The little brother replied that his Father always said that he was sure that Eddie was dead. When Eddie told him that he was the long lost brother, the little brother dropped his can of kerosene in the middle of the road and headed for home at a dead run to deliver the news.

Eddie told about one night when he was out drinking and driving in a little, light Model A Ford, which had poor lights, he felt a bump and thought he had run over an animal. He backed up, again felt the bump, and got out to find he had run over an acquaintance who was drunk. He examined the fellow and found him more drunk than hurt-- he had only run over his legs. He loaded the man into his car and took him home, cleaned him up, and helped him to sober up. The drunk was so appreciative of Eddie's picking him up and bringing him home that he remained a lifelong friend.

The drunk never did realize the true story, and Eddie surely never did tell him.

Eddie and a friend roomed together at a coal company

club house one time. The landlady got suspicious that some of the men were visiting the room of one of the hired girls at night, so she moved the girl to a room adjoining hers. This placed the girl's room real close to Eddie's and his friend's room in an ell, so that the windows of the two rooms were only five or six feet apart. One Saturday night, after a few drinks, Eddie decided to go visiting in the girl's room, so he placed a board on the two window sills and crossed over. After visiting for a while, he got up in the dark and started across the board. A voice from the bed inquired, "Who is it?" Eddie gave his roommate's name.

Occasionally I would help Eddie in the restaurant. Eddie liked to kid, but if it was more blessed to give than to receive, he was definitely blessed. One day the town errand boy came in and sat down on the stool at the counter. This young fellow shined shoes and did odd jobs for everyone, but he was not quite able to hold a full time job because of either mental or physical defects. Everyone teased him, and he got so that he had a reply to everything as he had heard the same things so often.

Eddie came in one day, slapped his hands on the counter and said, "Buck, are you getting any ---?" Buck, in a sour, grouchy voice growled, "No, why? Are you missing some?"

Eddie headed back into the kitchen and didn't reappear for a couple of hours.

STORIES I'VE HEARD

Mountain people used to entertain themselves when they met at stores, the post office and other meeting places by telling and re-telling incidents which had happened. Some were old stories, and some were new.

One story was about a mountain man who had a small hillside farm, but he had almost no equipment--nothing more complicated than a hoe, an axe and a crosscut saw. When the timber was beginning to be cut, and the lumbermen were paid by the number of board feet cut, this man decided to get in on the big wages. He got a young fellow for a buddy, bought a crosscut saw, axes, wedges and other necessary tools and got a job cutting timber. About the first day on the job, with all of this new equipment and tools, they started cutting timber.

They notched a tree and started sawing from the opposite side. When the saw started to bind, this man tapped his new wedge into the cut, and took a big swing with the sledge hammer to drive it deeper. His young partner didn't back out of the way far enough, and the back swing of the sledge hammer brushed his forehead enough to bring a trickle of blood.

The man looked around, saw what had happened, and advised his young partner, "Heck fire, boy, you've got to be kerful when you work around chinery."

Another story was told about the old mountain women who were meeting for a quilting bee. After having had ten to fifteen children and working fifteen hours a day for many years, they were utterly serious about everything they discussed. One day they were discussing a very small premature baby who was born to a young couple in the neighborhood. One woman remarked, "They say that when I was born I was so small they could place a wash pan over me." Another lady inquired, just as seriously, "Did you live?" The answer was just as serious. "They say that I lived and done well.'

They told of the mountain storekeeper who was sweeping his front porch one day when a young fellow and his girl friend drove up in a shiny convertible and stopped.

They were lost. The young man, in a smart alecky way, inquired, "Old man, how long before I get to civilization?" The store keeper, squinting down at him over his glasses, answered, "Young fellar, in your case, I'd say about twenty years."

The incident was told about the old timer who ran a small mountain hotel, which didn't do much business except during trout and hunting seasons, when he did a land office business. The night before deer season opened several people were checking in, including a man and his wife. The hotel keeper was straight laced and took no chances on hanky-panky, so, as usual for him, he asked for their marriage license. Naturally they didn't have one along, so the hunter dropped his hunting license on the counter and they went to their room. Later, when the hotel keeper had time to look things over better, he discovered the wrong license, and he immedicately headed up the stairs about three steps at a time. When he got to their door, he started yelling and pounding on their door, "If you haven't done it, don't do it, taint for it."

There was the story of the two men who had gone deer hunting back in the mountains in Pocahontas County. Along after noon they went looking for a place to eat, and the only place they could find was a small roadside cafe which did not look too clean, but they were left with no choice, so they went in and ordered lunch and glasses of water. One of the fellows, being very particular about cleanliness, said to the waitress, "Be sure that I have a clean glass." In a few minutes the waitress returned with two glasses of water and asked, "Now, which one of you wanted the clean glass?"

Many years ago a lady told this story about herself. Her husband's great uncle had died, and his funeral was to be in a little town a few miles away. Since her husband had to make a business call a few miles beyond this town, he asked her to drive her car to the funeral, and he would meet her there.

When she got to the funeral home she met a cousin from out of state, and she and her cousin decided that instead of going to the cemetery after the services, they would go to some other relatives home a few miles in the other direction. After the funeral they hurried to her car and, after some traffic problems, started out on a back road to visit. After a few miles she happened to push her big floppy hat back and discovered the hearse and the entire funeral procession following her, so she decided to speed up and lose them. She found she couldn't out run them, so she slowed down to let them pass. That didn't work either. Suddenly one car came around the whole procession, including her, and stopped. Her husband got out of his car, all upset, came back to her car and demanded to know, "Where in the hell are you taking Uncle Charley?"

There is a more recent story of an old man in Pocahontas County who went to apply for Social Security. During the interview the lady interviewer asked him for proof of his age. He was in his seventies, had a long white beard and looked ninety. She didn't question his age, but she still had to have actual proof. She asked him who could swear to his age, and he said his mother could. She was surprised and rattled and said, "Your mother? You've got a mother?" He exploded. 'Gol dang it, lady, have I got a mother? Even a rattlesnake has a mother."

The census taker who, pursuing his job through the hills and hollows of West Virginia, spotted a lonely cabin at the top of a high, rugged rise. Being a conscientious fellow, he puffed and sweated his way up the mountain. At the top, he stopped to get his breath before knocking on the cabin door. An old woman opened the door.

The census taker explained that he was from the government and was taking the census and would like to ask her some questions.

The woman said she wanted to help the government in any way she could, but she would like to know what he wanted to question her about. He said the government was trying to find out the exact population of the United States. She threw up her hand and cried, "God love you, honey, it wouldn't do you a bit of good to ask me. I don't have the slightest idea."